"Explain,"
said the machine.
"Describe their culture."

"They have an important celebration," said E.T., "called Hollow Bean. Everyone carves faces in fruit squashes and dresses up in sheets."

"Who holds this celebration?"

"The children, who actually rule the Blue Planet of Earth. They are more intelligent than the older people and outrun them on bicycles."

The machine whirled around him again. "And what is the purpose of this celebration?"

"To collect the all-important food."

"Which is?"

"Candy."

WEEKLY READER BOOKS PRESENTS

AN ILLUSTRATED NOVEL FOR YOUNG READERS

E.T.
THE BOOK OF
THE GREEN PLANET

a new novel by
WILLIAM KOTZWINKLE
based on a story by
STEVEN SPIELBERG

illustrations by
David Wiesner

BERKLEY BOOKS, NEW YORK

Permission to quote lyrics from "Kansas City" granted by Saul Halper, Halnat
Publishing Co., P.O. Box 37156, Cincinnati, Ohio 45222. Copyright 1958.
International copyright secured.

Lyrics from "Book of Love" by Warren Davis, George Malone, and Charles
Patrick: Copyright © 1957, 1958 Arc Music Corp. and Nom Music, Inc. All
rights controlled by Arc Music Corp. Reprinted by Permission. All Rights
Reserved.

Lyrics from "TUTTI FRUTTI" (Richard Penniman & Dorothy Labostrie)
© 1955, 1983 Venice Music, Inc. % ATV Music Corp., 6255 Sunset Boul-
evard, Hollywood, CA 90028. Used by Permission. All Rights Reserved.

Lyrics from "Johnny B. Goode" by Chuck Berry: Copyright © 1958 by Arc
Music Corp. Reprinted by Permission. All Rights Reserved.

E.T.

THE BOOK OF THE GREEN PLANET

AN ILLUSTRATED NOVEL FOR YOUNG READERS

A Berkley Book/published by arrangement with
MCA Publishing, a Division of MCA, Inc.

PRINTING HISTORY
Berkley edition/March 1985

ISBN: 0-425-08001-3

A BERKLEY BOOK® TM 757,375
Berkley Books are published by The Berkley Publishing Group,
200 Madison Avenue, New York, New York 10016.
The name "BERKLEY" and the stylized "B" with design
are trademarks belonging to Berkley Publishing Corporation.
PRINTED IN THE UNITED STATES OF AMERICA

CHAPTER ONE

"Catch it! Maintain contact!"

The spaceship gained steadily, while the jet planes strained at the edge of the atmosphere, shuddered, and turned their silver noses slowly over in defeat. The chase was abandoned, the ship beyond them now, rising still faster, a fading dot in the sky.

The Earth grew smaller as E.T. gazed from his porthole, his heart heavy at the sight of its diminishing shape, which fell like a blue-white tear drop, lost in the void. His friends were there— Elliott and Michael, Mary and Gertie, and Harvey the dog, and he would never see them again. "Goodbye," he whispered in a hoarse croak, "goodbye."

The tear drop vanished, swallowed by space. He stared dully out of the porthole, his mind automatically arranging and filing all that he knew of Earth, principally its language, which he'd nearly mastered, thanks to Elliott. He had chug-a-lugged the words, and could tee off any number of them, like a real shot-hot.

But words, and the lyrics to a few rocks and rolling songs were all he had. And a geranium.

He turned toward it. It was small, almost insignificant in the vast, wild array of growing things that filled his section of the ship.

He picked up the geranium and busied himself with it, making a place for it among the other plants of Earth that had been gathered; he made a tag for it, which, instead of saying *Geranium* said *Gertie,* a label that would cause some confusion in the Galactical Encyclopedia, but he didn't care. "B. good," he said, stroking the leaves, and continued on his rounds, among the other plants. The plants, exquisitely sensitive, perceived that a deep sadness had fallen on their beloved attendant, the celebrated Doctor of Botany.

1

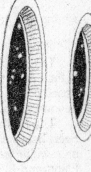

Another scholar of plant life entered the Botanical Wing, shuffling on webbed feet like E.T.'s. He shuffled over and put his hand on E.T.'s shoulder.

"Earth is not the only garden in the universe."

E.T. looked out of the porthole into empty space, and a name from the language of Earth broke from his wrinkled mouth. "Elliott!"

The other botanist looked around and scratched his head. No plant by that name had been brought on board. "What is the matter?"

E.T. turned from the porthole and gazed at his colleague. A look of deep longing crossed his face, as his lips parted again. "Wiped ... out."

Wiped out? The other old botanist ran the phrase through his memory bank of classic galaxy languages, but no connection was forthcoming, except for an image of someone drying the inside of a pot.

"But what did you do there that was so wonderful?"

"Ate candy."

E.T. turned back to the garden of the ship. A Whistling Ertmog, from a planet in the Andromeda Galaxy, whistled at him.

Cheer up, its song seemed to say, and the other plants in the central beds joined in, their waves of concern flowing over him.

"I made a true friend on Earth," he told the plants. "He saved my neck." And he raised his neck to its full height, to show the plants just how much saving it had taken. "We went through all kinds of doodleysquat together."

It was important he practice Earth language in the proper fashion, so as to speak like a sophisticated and learned thingamajig.

The door to the Botanical Wing opened, and a Micro Tech entered. Like all Micro Techs, he was very small, and his body was nearly transparent. His hands were his most peculiar feature, for the fingers were as tiny and numerous as hairs, and each hair could do microscopically detailed work. His eyes were enormous, and his face like a marble, smooth and shiny. He looked at E.T.

"Well, you're in trouble. Plenty of it."

E.T. watered his geranium. "I'm in trouble," he said softly. And then, remembering a phrase that Mary used when things went wrong, he added, "I'm in the soup."

We don't care, said the plants. *You are the best.*

"We are approaching the Dragon River of Stars," he said to the plants. "Within it is the Whirlpool of Time—first gate of dimension. The ship is already preparing for entry."

In a moment they would leave this continuum for another.

and he would lose Elliott forever, which was worse than being in the soup.

From the innermost centers of his mind and soul, a wave of telepathic intensity was released. It went down through Andromeda, between Aries and Pegasus, and into the solar system of Earth, where it spiraled in toward Elliott's part of the planet. Elliott was in a video arcade, throwing his last quarter to a machine on which he could never seem to score. He worked the joystick feverishly, missing every shot. E.T.'s telepathic wave came down, slightly off target, missing Elliott and landing in the back of the video machine. It perceived what Elliott wished, and began leaping around the circuits: Elliott's misfired salvos started scoring, one after another.

"Holy cow!"

The machine shifted to a more difficult level, and Elliott kept scoring, game after game, as lights and super sound effects started going off. "Highest score!" he shouted, blasting the last ship out of the screen.

In the midst of the electronic fireworks, fragments of invader ships arranged themselves into the shape of a pair of flickering letters—E T—but Elliott was too busy blasting away to notice. And in the next moment a certain girl passed through the video arcade.

"Hi, Elliott," she said, and Elliott felt a very odd sensation run through him, as if his knees had turned to soft ice cream and a bird had flown out of his heart.

He turned away from the machine, where E.T.'s message still flickered faintly, and he looked at—Julie. Her ponytail was tied with a little ring of rhinestones, which flickered in the light of the arcade.

He wanted to say something really cool and brilliant to her, maybe even remind her that he was the one who'd known the Extra-terrestrial. But he wasn't able to say anything cool or brilliant, because he'd just swallowed his gum while looking at her and it was lodged sideways in his throat. "Hi, Ju-lie," he croaked, but the noise of the arcade was so loud she seemed not to hear. Or maybe she heard and just pretended not to, which was a thing girls did. He was discovering that girls did *many* strange things, as strange and remote to Elliott as E.T. had been. "Girls are from another planet," he said to himself now, as he watched her walk on through the arcade.

He turned back to his game. And the message there, from another planet, had faded, and only ghostly spaceships moved across the screen.

*   *   *

E.T. sat in the botanical chamber, staring into Gertie's geranium. "This flower is Earth to me, and all happy memory."

His colleague, the other old botanist, looked up from his own work. He walked to the far wall and clicked a switch; a panel opened and a view screen appeared, out to the heavens. The Flower Nebula, pink-purple, floated before them, its masses of gas and stardust in petal-like arrangements.

E.T. gazed into the Flower Nebula. Within it was one of the greatest planets, whose appearance he could already discern— Mar'kinga Banda, giant planet, home of the super-strains of plant-life, whose trees towered into the clouds.

Its shape grew larger on the screen. "Yes, we're stopping there," said his colleague. "At Mar'kinga Banda, where the flowers are as big as this ship. You should prepare."

"Quite right," said E.T., his spirits lifting. "Mar'kinga Banda is a botanist's dream."

The ship sought its landing site and E.T. rushed with his colleague to the door leading from the Botanical Wing. His colleague stepped through, but when E.T. tried to follow, a Micro Tech intervened.

"Confined to quarters," smirked the superior little Tech, and began hooking up a weave of impassable light, bars of it, across the door.

E.T. had a bunk on one of the flower tiers and he climbed up into it now, and pulled the blanket over his head.

And he dreamed of the good times he'd had on Earth, living in a closet, eating candy, drinking beer, and wearing a wig. He saw Elliott and Michael, Mary, Gertie, and Harvey the dog, and he stayed asleep across the numberless eternities, dreaming of them, as his ship went about its many missions and finally— returned home.

CHAPTER TWO

Home—the Green Planet. As Earth was called the Blue Planet for its waters, so E.T.'s home was called the Green Planet for its plantlife, which flourished here as on no other planet in the world.

"Home, home, home." He paced about happily, chanting his favorite Earth word. And he thought that maybe there'd be a little band playing for him when he got off—for while he might be in the soup as far as the captain of the ship was concerned, the higher officials of the planet would certainly appreciate what he'd done—would recognize how important it was that he'd lived for weeks in a human closet.

The ship swept downward. It would no doubt land in one of the great capital cities and there the high lords would greet him; there the beings of light, far older than he, would make a party in his honor, for his achievements on Earth. He'd give a lecture on Earth language, social structure and science, unveiling all his advanced mind had gathered; also he'd show everyone how you had to have paper hats and whistles for a proper Earth party.

"Home, home, home." He saw a precious sight—the glow of one of the capitals, great Crystellum.

But the ship arced away from Crystellum, and sped on. Hapnod Illum, the second capital, appeared, but the ship also arced on over it, and it too fell behind. And then another and another, until the last great center, Lucidulum, was passed.

"They're taking you back," said the other old botanist, shuffling through the door.

"Back?"

"To the Farm."

The glow of Lucidulum faded, and the ship circled in over vast agricultural ranges, where the planet's food was grown. Here

E.T. had worked the soil for hundreds of years, learning its secrets as a simple farmer. He began to recognize the terrain, from which he'd graduated long ago, after very hard exams, following which he'd become a full-fledged intergalactical Doctor of Botany. And now—

"Demoted," said his colleague.

"To the bush league," said E.T., remembering how they would shout this on Earth TV each Saturn Day, when the man waving a stick too often missed the white sphere—*send him back to the bush league.* Also to be heard was the cry, *Send him to the showers!* He'd been sent to the showers on Earth, and it had almost killed him, lying there with Elliott, water running over him. That was when he'd been so sick, and he sincerely hoped he'd never be sent to the showers again.

The signal for landing filled the ship, and a moment later it settled down, in the bush. The outer hatch opened automatically, and he went down the gangplank, onto the soil of the Green Planet.

The ship lifted off, and he stepped backward, away from its radiance. At the porthole of the Botanical Wing, he saw a face— that of his colleague, waving sadly. E.T. waved back, his fingertip glowing with a feeble light.

Which way was he to go? He began to walk, not caring where his footsteps took him. But before he'd gone far, a small local range cruiser came hurtling through the sky toward him. A moment later it was hovering before him, and the metallic petals of its hatchway opened. *"Enter,"* came the command from within.

He entered, and the petals immediately closed behind him. He was enclosed in a cubicle room. One of its walls opened, and a smaller cube rolled out on wheels; twin antennae emerged from its top surface and a bank of lights flashed across its face. "Explain," said a mechanical voice from within it.

"I tried to b. good," said E.T.

"Not good enough." The interrogation machine wheeled around him, antennae quivering, as if examining him from all sides.

"I met the people of Earth," said E.T.

"We know. Please make your report." The voice of the machine was remote, superior, and E.T. knew it had been programmed by someone high in the planetary command. Would they try to confuse him, to be sure he wasn't making anything up? He looked down into his geranium and tried to collect his thoughts. Where could he possibly begin?

"Come, come," said the machine. "Describe their culture."

"They have an important celebration called Hollow Bean. Everyone carves faces in fruit squashes and dresses up in sheets. I myself dressed in one."

"Who holds this celebration?"

"The children, who actually rule the Blue Planet of Earth. They are much more intelligent and sensitive than the older people and outrun them on bicycles." E.T. nodded into his geranium. He was getting the facts straight, and the high command would learn much from his report, for inclusion in the Galactical Encyclopedia.

The machine circled around him again. "And what is the purpose of this celebration?"

"To collect the all-important food, which is candy."

"Candy?"

"D. licious," said E.T.

The machine paused, an odd buzzing sound coming from inside it, as if it was having difficulty assimilating information. Finally, its voice resumed: "Did you meet the ruler of Earth?"

"Elliott."

"Elliott is the ruler? How old is he? Has he ten-thousand years?"

"He's ten."

"Ten? And he rules?"

The machine's lights blinked violently, and this was followed by more static buzzing. "Did the people of Earth acknowledge the advanced nature of your intellect?"

"They kept me in what is called a closet, where the most prized possessions are kept, among them Kermit the Frog, and a collection of illustrated works on the life of the great Flash Gourd On."

E.T. began to breathe more easily. The interview was going well, without confusion.

"And what form of enlightenment did you give these young rulers?"

"We drank beer and stole things. The police chased us and many objects in our way got creamed."

"Creamed?"

"A special Earth word," said E.T. "I know many such now."

The machine buzzed with confusion again, rolled forward, then backward, then bumped into a wall. It rotated slowly toward him. "Depart."

The hatchway opened and E.T. shuffled back out, holding his geranium. He felt the debriefing had been very successful and now that they knew how much valuable information about Earth he'd brought, they'd call him back up from the league of bushes.

The petal hatchway of the cruiser closed, and the vessel rose up, and sped away, leaving him deep in the outer agricultural ranges, alone, to figure things out, which he did, immediately.

"Creamed," he said to himself, and began to walk along, toward the old Farm.

*   *   *

The path ran over hills and through forests. The trees were mostly Jumpums, of great vigor. The entire family of Jumpum trees took short hops every so often, and then dug their roots like frenzied claws deep into the soil.

A bunch of Jumpums jumping all around you, if you're not used to them, can be upsetting, and E.T. scolded a few of them for jumping almost on top of him, their roots pinning his long toes in place. "B. good."

They looked at him sadly, their leaves drooping to the ground as they backed off, for he was a distinguished botanist and they were just silly young Jumpums.

"I'm sorry," he said, and jumped around with them for a while to make them feel better; his short legs did not get him far in the jumping category but the Jumpums didn't care, and jumped merrily. He left them as they started to organize a jumping contest, which was much too strenuous for anyone but a Jumpum. He walked on, carrying his geranium, as evening fell.

A few more steps brought him out of the forest, and into a field. In it a solitary figure worked at the end of day, bent over a long cultivated row. He looked much like E.T. but his neck did not seem able to raise itself as high.

"A youngster," said E.T. to himself. "Only several hundred years old. Doing the work I once did."

The youthful creature was tending a crop of Beeperbeans, which gave off a sharp beeping sound when their blossoms opened. As it was springtime, there was considerable beeping going on, and the worker had corks in his ears.

I'll just give him a little surprise...

E.T. was beside the youngster before he knew it, and when the little fellow turned, a cry sprang from his lips and the corks popped out of his ears.

"Excuse me, Doctor," he said, addressing E.T. by his proper title. "I didn't know—*beep*—you were—*beep beep*—making your rounds—*beep.*"

"Proceed," said E.T., not wanting to admit to this mere child that he'd soon be tending Beeperbeans himself, and hear beeps in his sleep, and talk in beeps, and nearly be a beep, before spring was complete.

But then he paused, and said to the youngster, "Let me show you a trick with the Beeperbean, one that will reduce your discomfort."

He took the youngster to the nearby wood and pointed out an herb called Noorf-og-inki, or Essence of Pure Silence. "Nothing can completely subdue a beeperbean, of course, for they are so exuberant, but a few pinches of this in the nutrient flow will quiet them considerably."

"My deep-beep-est gratitude, Doctor," said the student botanist. "It will save my eardrums and... beep beep... my sanity ... beep. For I confess to beep-being half-crazed and beep-becoming worse every hour."

"Yes, well, I also suggest... beep... suggest you discard the corks from your ears and use beep-beeswax instead. It's much beep-beep-better."

"Thank you, Doctor, for beep-befriending."

"Not at all. But now I must beep-be leaving you. So, b.beep good."

He crested the hill and a vast patchwork of fields appeared before him in the reddish bronze of evening. He crossed the spine of the hill, and saw another familiar sight—one of the pocket

villages used by the workers who attended the surrounding fields.

The village, like the fields, was an organic thing, a hybrid—for the cottages of the agriculturalists had not been built, but grown. A little biochemistry and some saturated nutrients had produced a species of gourd called Chemon Xrus, meaning Big Enough To Live In.

E.T. hurried down the slope toward the ring of giant gourds, his heart-light glowing. From one of the gourds, an answering light came from a window. He ran up the path to the gourd, the door of which was now glowing all around the edges.

It swung open before E.T., and he entered.

Standing within was a creature like E.T., but tall and stately. The creature's heart-light was brilliant, ablaze with wisdom.

"Parent," said E.T. softly, and approached with hesitant step.

"Well, child, you certainly made a mess of things."

The great Parent was sighing, with a slow shake of its noble head; but then a long arm reached out and embraced E.T. Hearts merged, saying things for which there are no words.

The gourd was lit by Lumens, a species of large phosphorescent grub. Five or six Lumens gave quite enough light to read by, a nice even glow falling all around.

"So," said the Parent, when they were seated facing each other in the chamber, "what exactly did you do on Earth?"

"Peeked in windows."

"Peeked in windows? You? A Botanist of the Capital, First Class?"

"In all the history of the planet there is no one who has goofed as badly as I have."

"You always were too curious," said the Parent.

"True, too true."

The Parent sighed again. "You traveled from one end of the universe to the other, you saw a thousand worlds, worlds few creatures are privileged to see—great, unexplainable systems of astounding beauty, teeming with amazing sights to behold—and you had to go peek in a window."

CHAPTER THREE

He's back, he's back!

This one thought was racing through the head of a creature known scientifically as the Igigi Gyrum Hadahadeba, meaning Six-hundred Vertebrae In The Spine. But everyone on the Green Planet just called them Flopglopples, for one of their modes of travel was to flop around like a long gloppy length of something. They perhaps resembled most closely a pile of gray floppy socks. They were very fast, very agile, very stupid, and very loving. And this particular one was devoted to E.T.

"Back, he's back in our system of reference so we can now say he is here now whereas before we couldn't say he was anywhere now because he was thirty-eight light-years away quite beyond the now."

There are some Green Planet scientists who say that Flopglopples are old and very wise. However, this has never been proven, as Flopglopples enjoy giving silly answers on intelligence tests.

A moment more and he was speeding through the village, green gravel flying out from underneath his tripod of flopping feet. He raced past the sign saying *Flopglopples Slow Down,* and sent gravel up against a number of window panes.

He skidded to a stop in front of E.T.'s cottage, ran around it excitedly, and finally flopped in over a windowsill, as it was opened and the door was not. A millisecond later he was flopped around E.T.'s shoulders, draped like a stole and hugging him devotedly.

"B. good," said E.T., as the Flopglopple hung upside down, looking him in the eyes with a smile.

"Let us dine," said the Parent, and poured from the pitcher

plant beaker, into the blossom cups. The liquid was ambrosial, with all needed nutrients, and was served with biscuits similarly constituted, but E.T. could not help thinking the repast was not in the same class as a handful of Reese's Pieces and a bottle of beer. However, he thanked the Parent, gave some ambrosia and biscuit to the Flopglopple, and sat back on the couch, gazing out at the lighted village. In many ways, it beat living in a closet. But still, there was a tug within him.

El-li-ott, he said softly to himself, and a telepathic wave went out from between his brows, pierced the roof of the gourd, and then streaked on its way. The little telepathic replicant arrived on Earth in the middle of a shopping mall, on the fast food counter, and the tiny telepathic replicant, in every way resembling E.T., landed in the mustard bowl. He climbed out, and was struck by a plastic tray, which knocked him down the counter into the cash register. It opened with a bang behind him and sent him flying into the ice cream blender.

As he was whirling around in the cream, the little tele-replicant got the feeling that someone he knew was near.

In fact, Elliott's mother, Mary, was seated at the counter on her lunch hour, wondering: "Why am I about to eat a hamburger, two hot dogs, a double order of french fries, a milk shake, and a cupcake covered with dyed candy sprinkles?"

She looked into her milk shake and saw, fleetingly, a little wrinkled being, floating in the foam.

Then she looked down at her cupcake, where the tiny candy sprinkles were arranging themselves and spelling M A R Y.

She tapped the mall janitor on the back. "Sir, would you please tell me what's written on this cupcake?" She held it up to him.

"You've been shoppin' too long, lady. I seen it before. Go home, relax."

She turned and saw Elliott coming down the hallway of the mall. How unfortunate that he was going to see his own mother stuffing herself with the very foods she tried to pretend she never ate.

"Hi, Mom," he said. "Pigging out?"

"Yes, dear."

"Mom, did you see any friends of mine around? I just had the funniest feeling that somebody I knew was here."

"Sorry, Elliott, I haven't seen anyone."

"I keep having the feeling I told someone I'd meet them here at the fast food place."

"Well, did you?"

"No." He looked at her cupcake. "I'd better help you out, Mom," he said, and grabbed it from her plate. She thought of grabbing it back but decided a mother should not be seen fighting with her son over pastry in a public place. And in any case, Elliott didn't even give her the chance. He was already moving off down the hallway of the mall, following a pretty little girl with a rhinestoned ponytail.

CHAPTER FOUR

"You should report to the fields," said the Parent.

E.T. nodded. The faithful Flopglopple went out of his gourd with him, onto the gravel path.

"This way," said E.T., taking a back path. "I don't want to meet anyone."

"Why not?"

"Because I'm in disgrace."

"Oh, that's nothing," said the Flopglopple. "I'm always in disgrace for racing through villages and otherwise acting up."

The Flopglopple ran ahead, teasing the ancient lizards of the forest, who looked at him with slitted eyes, and then looked at E.T., tongues flickering in a whisper.

Get this Igigi Gyrum out of here.

E.T. attempted to restrain the Flopglopple. "Never tease lizards."

"They're so stiff and scaly," said the Flopglopple. "I can't help myself." He tweaked the distinguished reptiles by the tails, then vanished in a whirl of leaves and dust. E.T. followed, to the forest's edge. Before him were the fields, stretching to the horizon. From them, morning vapors arose, and through the mist that hugged the rows he saw the agriculturalists moving—creatures like himself, but all young, much younger, their knowledge just beginning to form.

"While mine is complete. A complete fool."

But thoughts of his folly on Earth made him long for his friend there, and a tele-beam went out from his forehead and headed for Earth. The little tele-replicant of E.T. came down, almost on target, in Elliott's classroom.

It was a computer class, and the little replicant landed in Elliott's machine. Seeing a good opportunity at hand, the tele-replicant began creating a message from within the computer. A single word, telling all, flashed on Elliott's screen:

Owch

But Elliott was looking across the aisle at a certain young lady he'd grown strangely attracted to lately—for Elliott had grown in years since the time E.T. had left. Time-travel distorts and while E.T. had aged little, Elliott had grown and entered junior high school—and found new interests there.

Such as this girl, whose long ponytail fascinated him in ways he could not quite explain.

Owch Owch Owch

said the screen. But Elliott's head was still turned.

"All right, class," said the teacher. "Clear your machines."

Elliott, still looking at the young lady, pressed a single button, and E.T. was wiped out of memory.

*   *   *

E.T. stood at the edge of the agricultural fields. The young workers there drew back deferentially as he approached, for they could feel his higher mind, and they could see for themselves how the plants were responding to E.T.'s presence—buds opening as if to greet him.

Then E.T. himself felt a higher wave, far higher than his own, the wave length of his teacher—Botanicus.

Botanicus appeared. His form was like the Parent—tall and slender. His walk was slow and stately, and a large jade-skinned lizard accompanied him, forked tongue flickering as he waddled along beside his master.

Botanicus gestured to the plants, all ten of his fingertips glowing with the marks of the Adept.

"Each shining fingertip," said E.T. softly to the students, "represents an achievement of wisdom so great that it glows, and is with him always, as a power at his command."

As Botanicus gestured, as the light streamed from his fingers, new shoots appeared all along the row, buds multiplied, and leaves that had been scarred by insects were healed.

Most learned, Supreme Scientist, Lord of the Fields—Botanicus.

"Prize pupil." He extended his hand to E.T. "Come here, pride and joy."

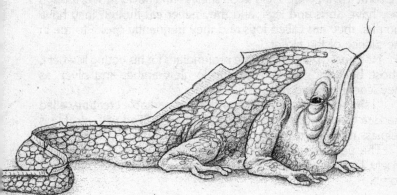

E.T. moved in front of him. Botanicus put his leathery palm on E.T.'s head and closed his eyes. "Sap down in the toes. What's wrong?"

"Weeded out," said E.T. "Kicked off the ship."

"Come," said Botanicus, and gestured for them to follow him, deeper into the fields.

The gardens of Botanicus contained many bizarre creations, the most unusual of which, perhaps, was the agi Jabi. One of them stood at the end of the row, a tall plant, something like corn, but which had been crossed with a Jumpum and a Shrieking Ja— to produce a plant who guarded the field from marauding birds. If birds came by, the agi Jabi leapt out, waved its stalks and produced a deafening cry, after which it would go back to its silent vigil. Like most hybrids, it was temperamental and shrieked at everyone who came along—except for Botanicus, whom it recognized and loved.

So the morning passed, as they tended the rows, and then, when it was time for a rest, they followed Botanicus into a grove of Fluteroots, where the music of the wind played softly through hollow reeds and everyone gathered around the teacher.

"Tell us of your adventures on Earth," said Botanicus, turning to E.T.

"Earth has many strange creatures," he began. "Most strange are some I lived with. They sit on shelves and never move, though they have arms and legs, and they never eat though they have mouths, they are called *toys* and they frequently spoke to me in the silence of the closet."

He paused, to gather more profundities for his young listeners, whose head-moss was beginning to glow amber and silver, as they leaned toward him.

"I shared my quarters with another remarkable creature called the Baa Sket Ba, who is a little round being filled with air. He is helpless to go anywhere unless you bounce him."

The young workers' mouths had fallen open. E.T. nodded wisely, happy to be educating them to the way of worlds far from home.

*   *   *

E.T. worked all day beside the others, at jobs he hadn't done for ages. His Flopglopple, after running amok in the rows for several hours, settled down beside him to help with the soil test. "We're back on the job," he said to E.T. affectionately.

"Yes," said E.T., "it is pleasant work." But his head kept turning skyward, sunward and beyond, and a mental wave went out, jumped universes, and found Earth.

It came down in a row of phone booths near the school bus stop, where Elliott and his friends had gathered. E.T.'s tele-replicant got twisted up in the telephone currents, its message spiraling out and into the ear of a salesman using the phone.

"Hello, Mother, this is Sheldon . . . no, I'm not in jail. Mother, please, I don't need a loan, I'm selling underwear. Does Dad need any boxer shorts? No, that's not why I'm calling, I don't *know* why I'm calling, I suddenly had this urge to *phone home.*"

Elliott climbed into the school bus. He'd sit with his friends and pretend he hadn't noticed Julie get on. When dealing with girls you had to pretend right back—that you didn't care about them, that you'd rather be punching a friend, or shouting hysterically. That was the way it was done; that was the only way to get someplace with girls—to go no place at all.

He couldn't help wondering if there wasn't something basically incorrect about the procedure.

CHAPTER FIVE

The Ios Naba, or Contentment Monitor, was streaking along—a whirlpool of multicolored light whose center resembled an eye. Its job was to see that everyone was happy. It flew over the fields from row to row, then zipped into E.T.'s row. It expanded its whirling pool of color until it had enveloped E.T.

"Something's wrong. Can't have that. Tell your Contentment Monitor all about it. You'll feel much better."

"I miss my friend."

"Fine, I'll get him." The Contentment Monitor pointed itself. "Where is he?"

E.T. pointed upward. "Beyond the beyond."

"Odd place for a friend."

E.T. stared sadly into the whirling eye. How could he explain that friends are arranged by fate, and distance nothing? "He is very special."

"How?"

E.T. thought a moment, then said, "He introduced me to Gum."

"Who is Gum?"

"Gum is a wizard. Great Gum permitted me to blow bubbles in which dreams are seen." E.T. elongated his neck, head rising up. "Gum's world is beautiful, I saw much inside his bubble before it exploded all over my face."

The Contentment Monitor's whirl intensified. *Must do something here,* it said to itself. *Have to cheer this fellow up, get him smiling again. A bubble, eh?*

A large multicolored bubble rose from the Monitor's whirling form. "How do you like *that?*" asked the Monitor proudly.

23

"Truly wonderful," said E.T., not wanting to hurt the Monitor's feelings.

"So you feel better now?"

"Much better."

"Excellent," said the Monitor, and whirled away. *Not a very tough case at all. I wonder what the Contentment Council could have meant when they said the Doctor of Botany was deeply troubled?*

*   *   *

Down the long neck of the gourd he walked, carrying a string of Lumens, the little glowing grubs dangling in the air before him and lighting the way. His room was in the neck of the gourd, at the very end, and was quite small.

He climbed into bed, closed his eyes, and immediately a beam shot from his forehead. The little replicant beam streaked past the million mighty suns, and down to Earth, into an all-night pizza parlor. The replicant fumbled around, wondering what it was doing in the anchovies, then corrected its trajectory and streaked off down the block toward Elliott's house.

Elliott, asleep, felt his own dream suddenly expanding, into an ever-widening sphere, inside of which he stood, gazing at curving walls. He peered through the thin sticky membrane and saw that he was floating above the bright lights of a city. Then suddenly the bubble rose higher, the city grew smaller, and a gravelly voice croaked, *"Have some Gum."*

"E.T.!"

The dream bubble popped, and Elliott sat up in bed in the lonely darkness.

"E.T.," he said softly, but there was no one there.

*   *   *

"Morning exercises!" said the Flopglopple, stretching. "Isometrics, hard as I can." He stretched his arms out and they simply elongated, no tension possible in them, so flexible were his skin and all his joints. "Ah, that feels much better." He snapped them back to normal length.

"You are an odd creature."

"My brain is loosely hinged," answered the Flopglopple. "Sometimes it slips into my toes."

"We must go to work," said E.T., and led the Flopglopple into the garden of the Trompayd plant.

The shiny Trompayd petals opened to the sun and the entire row of Trompayds let out a deafening blast, brassy and bright, to greet the sunrise.

"Owch!" cried E.T., holding his ears, as the Trompayd blossoms quivered, cheek-like petals blown out toward the sun as they trompayded.

In the distance, a faint drumming sounded, from the hill of the Timpanum plants. This signal, of Trompayd and Timpanum, quickened all the gardens of the morning, powers waking, soil humming, and E.T. felt his secret fate quickening too.

"Why must I be the planetary rebel?" he asked the Flopglopple.

"Perhaps you are like me," said the Flopglopple. "You enjoy stirring things up."

"But I don't. I like smoothing things over. I like my feet up on a sofa, eating peanuts." A thought-wave went out of his head, toward Earth.

The wave connected with Elliott, in an alley behind his school, where a ring of boys had gathered. Elliott was in the center of the ring, fists up, and an angry look in his eyes.

"G'wan, Elliott, knock his block off."

The circle closed, and Elliott's opponent came after him, fists flying. Elliott felt the blows land, but he didn't feel E.T.'s thought-wave land, though it made a direct hit in the center of his forehead. He was too busy hitting his opponent.

E.T., light-years away, closed his eyes and wondered why Elliott couldn't hear, when the beam had struck so directly on center.

The Flopglopple looked at E.T., and listened in on the communication. "Growing up."

"What?" E.T., startled, looked at the Flopglopple.

"Getting older," said the Flopglopple, and resumed his digging.

"Growing up, growing up, growing up." E.T. paced the row,

terribly upset, for when people on Earth grew up they lost their wisdom. On the Green Planet, here in the Seventh Nebula of Galactus, as you grew up you got wiser. On Earth, for some reason, when young creatures matured, they lost their secret rulership and became slaves, fools, and blew each other to pieces. He'd seen it on the 6:30 news.

"My friend is in danger. He is about to become the most terrible thing of all. He is about to become Man."

CHAPTER SIX

The maintenance depot was run exclusively by Micro Techs, and at the depot's heart was the Micro Tech Club, where the frenzied little beings went to unwind; its dome was decorated with bands of colored laser light, and music could be heard coming from its windows.

"I'm trying to restrain myself," said the Flopglopple, his tripod of feet scratching frantically in the ground. "But I *can't!*" And he raced toward the Club, went through the doorway in a blinding rush, and disappeared within.

E.T. approached more slowly.

"Well," he said to himself as he came to the doorway. "I've *got to party.*" With this Earth phrase to brace him, he squared his shoulders and entered.

Tables were crowded around a small dance floor, where the Flopglopple was already gyrating with other Igigi Gyrums, their little slender bodies snapping madly, their tripodial feet moving in a blur. Music came from a gleaming little bandstand, and there a Fluteroot was swaying, playing its heart out; it was accompanied by a Trompayd, the Trompayd's brassy golden cheek petals swelling out as it blew. A pair of Timpanurns, their taut drumhead blossoms thumping like rhythmic hearts, kept an intricate beat. The plants were all potted, in large containers provided by the management.

E.T. skirted the dance floor, where a handful of young Jumpums were bouncing up and down to the beat; they came to the Club in their early years, before they grew too big to get through the door.

E.T. made his way to the bandstand. The Fluteroot tooted

27

above him, swaying in its pot, and the Trompayd bent back, blowing a high sweet passage. Seated on the stalk of the Trompayd was a Micro Tech, playing the fifty string a'lud, each string as thin as a hair; his own hair-like fingers, countless in number, picked over the strings in a blur, producing the most intricate sound imaginable.

This was Micron, the only Micro Tech E.T. was friendly with, from a voyage made long ago, to a planet whose musical enchantments had affected Micron and changed him, and made him an outsider. His fifty string a'lud was from that planet, and remained the source of his enchantment.

"I hear you've had bad luck," said Micron.

"It's probably going to get worse."

"Why?"

E.T. lifted his long neck, craning it high and looking around to see if he might be overheard. Then he lowered it and leaned in toward Micron. "I'm going to borrow a starcruiser."

CHAPTER SEVEN

"This is the region of the ancient mines," said E.T. "Why have you brought us here?"

Micron said nothing, only smiled and led the way into the hills. Stone piles, from early excavations, lay everywhere. It was a barren place, dead as an airless moon. "From another time," said the Flopglopple, "in the beginning."

"I'm receiving a signal," said E.T., "a dark one."

"From there," said Micron, and pointed to a shadow in the hillside. As they approached, E.T. saw it was the opening to one of the abandoned mines, millennia old.

But just beyond the shadow of the opening was a heavy metallic seal, blocking the shaft from entry.

"Locked," said the Flopglopple.

Micron studied it for a moment, then ran his spidery fingers over the face of the plate. "One of the old electron locks, simple enough if you know how." His fingers worked, emitting a steady stream of squeaks and beeps of the electron code. The plate grew suddenly incandescent, and itself began to squeak and beep, and a moment later it became transparent, and then vanished altogether.

A dank, damp smell rose from the passageway.

Micron drew a laser torch from his little tool case, and it cast a bright beam into the darkness ahead.

"There's the old descent tube," he said, pointing to a circular shape in the rock ahead of them. Dust and webs covered it, dulling a finish that had once been bright.

Micron ran his fingers over the face of the descent tube and a control panel popped open, cobwebs and dust flying up from it.

"Well, come aboard." A door swung open in the tube, more dusty webs breaking apart. E.T. and the Flopglopple stepped inside. E.T. felt an almost imperceptible movement, but a glance at the gauge showed they were descending at a very high speed.

The Flopglopple looked around with great interest and saw a distortion of himself on the curving inner wall, head greatly elongated. "Pressure P on corresponding volume V?" He pointed at his head, thinking it had actually shaped itself into a cone, which he thought very handsome.

"A reflection," said E.T.

"Reflection," mused the Flopglopple, but kept feeling his dome hopefully, as the descent continued.

And then, smoothly, it stopped. The door opened and they stepped out.

They stood in a rock gallery, whose roof arched high overhead; at the far end of the gallery, light and shadow moved.

"Who visits?" A figure moved from the shadows.

Micron stepped forward. "We come as friends," he said, voice echoing through the gallery.

"Friends?" The figure took a step forward. "We have no friends. Approach cautiously, intruders."

"But where are your arms?" asked the Flopglopple, perhaps impolitely, and staring at the creature's odd-shaped body—a long, mummy-like cylinder of blue and purple, faceted as was his head.

E.T. saw that his eyes reflected lost dreams, of the former eon, when metallic beings had ruled, and gathered the metals of the moons and the diamonds of the comets, and ravaged the planetary system with war.

Sudden apprehension filled E.T. More trouble would result from conspiring with such a being. I'm liable to find myself in a jam, a pickle, and the dog home.

"We need a flight crew," said Micron, "to get us through the warp of time. And you've piloted big ships in the past."

The old miner studied his guests more closely now, and an orange-yellow luster filled the crystal lattice of his eyes. "I am called Occulta. I used to fly the great starcruisers of the former eon. And I'm at your service." He smiled, and a drop of mercurial substance dripped from his lips.

* * *

Occulta took them deeper, down a corridor of hewn pillars.
"Another being ahead," said the Flopglopple.

E.T. studied the armless shape. Where had he seen such a thing before?

"A large bulb of garlic," said the Flopglopple, examining the rotund sheaths of the creature, each of them like a separate clove. But instead of the fragile skin of that plant, the creature's skin was armor plate, and no knife could ever peel it, that was certain.

"I am Sinistro. What business have you here?"

"They wish to recruit us," interjected Occulta. "To pilot them through the warp of time. We know it well, eh, Sinistro?"

They laughed together then, and suddenly their bodies expanded, blossoming outward in the most astonishing way. The metallic folds lifted, like petals, raised from within by long thin arms, hidden until now.

I must be cautious, said E.T. to himself, for many a jam pickle could result.

"B. good." He raised his finger gently toward the old asteroid miner.

Occulta and Sinistro led the way to a chamber where the last of the subterraneans dwelled.

I am Electrum, said a telepathic voice.

The crystal eyes sparkled and Electrum rose. He stepped toward his visitors, and the Flopglopple rushed to examine him. "A toadstool without a stem," said the Flopglopple, studying Electrum's squat shape. "Yes, with an umbos on top." The Flopglopple was pointing, rudely perhaps, at Electrum's bullet-shaped head, growing out of his mushroom-like body.

"Welcome—to the depths."

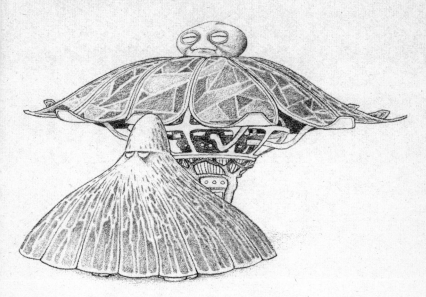

All three of the beings expanded together, their metallic folds lifting like flowers. Their bodies glowed now, as their arms gestured in the lost signing of long ago. Occulta, Sinistro, and Electrum conversed in silence, and then, once more, their metallic sheaths were lowered and their wild forces were concealed.

"So—you have your crew."

CHAPTER EIGHT

The starcruiser sat on its launch pad in the moonlit valley, in the hills beyond Lucidulum. Micro Techs swarmed over the cruiser, attending to its needs.

"Ants," snarled Sinistro, "crawling over a shiny apple."

"That's the Matter Converter they're working on," said Micron.

"Photon rocket." Sinistro lay beside him in their hiding post in the hills. "Design hasn't changed much since the old days."

"Yes," said Occulta, "we know it well."

Electrum moved his toadstool-like body along the edge of their hiding place, so he could see the aft portion of the ship. "Our old designs have never been bettered. That ship can travel forever, refueling itself from the matter of the stars."

Then, at a window in a section of the ship most familiar to E.T.—the Botanical Wing—a face like his own appeared.

"Owch," said E.T. softly, as he saw his fellow botanist in the position he himself once held, off to gather the flowers of space, for the universal garden.

The ship rose and E.T.'s thoughts went with it, in a telepathic signal soaring through the heavens. It navigated the labyrinths of stars, and came down, nearly on target. Elliott was at the park pool, getting set to show off with a fancy dive. Julie was seated at the edge of the pool, legs splashing back and forth in the water. Her bathing cap was shaped like layers of flower petals, and E.T.'s little replicant landed in them, thinking she was a large white rose. A funny feeling went through her, as the replicant touched her, a feeling of something faraway and strange. And it had to do with—Elliott.

35

She turned toward him. He walked to the edge of the diving board, sprang off, and came down flat on his back with a loud *splat,* and sank like a stone.

Julie pushed off the edge of the pool and swam over to him as he surfaced, glassy-eyed.

"Are you alright?" she asked.

Water was running out of his nose, ears, and mouth. "Sure, sure," he gasped. "I was just—experimenting. Testing the board."

"Are you going to test it again?" she asked, teasingly, as he held on to the ladder, still gasping for breath.

"Yeah," he said, for he *did* have one more fancy dive in his repertoire, where he grabbed his knees and went in like a bowling ball. He wished he were a swimmer, a great swimmer. Oh, if only I had a teacher.

El-li-ott, cried the little replicant, fighting against the pull of the drain, and thrashing in the water.

Elliott turned his head, but there was no one there, only a few rainbow reflections glittering on the water's tossing surface.

"Let's swim together," said Julie. "We'll do the sidestroke."

"Sure, fine," said Elliott. That was the stroke in which he sank sideways and got chlorine up just one nostril, an old favorite. He gazed at her and wished he had the guts to play a big love scene, but it was better to remain hard-to-get, so he rolled over and switched to his Olympic backstroke, the one where he sank *gradually,* like a submarine.

Nearby, the little replicant fought with its own best stroke against the suction of the drain, but it was caught in the whirling water and filtered out of the pool.

*   *   *

E.T. entered the transparent dome. Row after row of exceedingly odd plantlife was displayed, and the air was heavy with scent. "This," said E.T. to the Flopglopple, "is where Botanicus raises his rarest blossoms."

The oddest plant in the hothouse had two especially long branches that hung into the dirt like arms, and the rest of its shape gave the impression of someone very tired, asleep against a post;

the uppermost blossom, in fact, emitted a tiny snoring sound, petals moistly fluttering. From this blossom, E.T. took a tiny pinch of pollen, a disturbance which caused the plant to shift, like a person turning over in bed, but the snoring continued.

"And what brings you here, Doctor?" The voice of Botanicus came softly behind E.T., who popped into the air with a little jolt of surprise. He turned and slipped the bit of pollen to his Flopglopple, who took it, and slid back under a bench, out of the reach of Botanicus.

"I've got to—buzz off," said E.T.

"Are you a bee?"

Botanicus stepped closer, but E.T. was already out the door, and proceeding down the path with his Flopglopple, who still held the handful of pollen in his palm.

"What is this?" he asked E.T.

"It's from the Shemoda Nuncoor, the Sleeping Princess Plant."

"And what does its pollen do?" The Flopglopple brought his fingertip to his smiling mouth, and a second later he was asleep on his feet, toes pointed out. A loud snore broke from his lips and he swayed back and forth, and finally crumpled to the ground.

*   *   *

"So, Doctor," said Sinistro to E.T., "what's on this planet Earth to which you so desperately want to go? What kind of treasure can we expect?"

"One day you might have your own—closet."

"I would like that," said Sinistro, pretending he understood. "Indeed, I cannot wait to have my own closet."

"And a football helmet."

"Yes, naturally, I must have one of those."

Electrum leaned forward, eyes flashing. "What about me?"

"You might have your own TV set," said E.T.

"Truly wonderful," said the dark lord.

Occulta leaned toward E.T. "And I? What shall I have?"

"Your own bicycle," said E.T.

Occulta nodded, not wishing to appear ignorant before his colleagues. "That's as it should be. Good, very good."

38   WILLIAM KOTZWINKLE

* * *

"I dreamed we had a spaceship," said the Flopglopple, "but it was a strange one."

"Shhhhhhh," said E.T.

The Flopglopple put a finger to his own lips, and reminded himself to be quiet. "Shhhhhhh."

Ahead were several square acres of paddy, where a refined substance grew—a hybrid of Bazmat Lizoona, Brain Plant of the Jungle, and food of the starcruiser launch base.

"Bazmat Lizoona," said E.T., quietly addressing the spirit of the paddy, "I've brought a new nutrient for you—Shemoda Nuncoor, the Sleeping Princess." He emptied the pollen pouch into the arms of Bazmat Lizoona. An ecstatic tremble ran through the gelatinous substance of the paddy.

"A new hybrid has just been made," said E.T. to the Flopglopple.

"And tomorrow the base will dine on it," said the Flopglopple.

"Yes," said E.T. excitedly, and a telepathic beam rose from his brain, and found its way to Earth. It landed in the TV section of a department store, where twenty-five TV screens suddenly showed a silvery ghost, with duck feet and a long neck, crowned by an eggplant-shaped head.

"Come on, Gertie, we've got to buy you some galoshes."

A familiar voice sounded in the aisles. The telepathic replicant turned, little neck rising up, toward Mary, as she dragged Gertie along.

"I don't *want* galoshes," said Gertie. "We don't even *call* them galoshes anymore."

"What do you call them?"

"Designer boots."

"Well, *I'm* calling them galoshes," said Mary.

"I hate them."

"You'll learn to love them. All little girls learn to love their galoshes."

"Only if they're yellow. And I'm not little anymore."

"Sir, do you have any yellow galoshes?"

"No, madam."

"See," said Gertie.

"Please, Gertie, be cooperative, we're going to buy *green* galoshes."

"Yuck."

"Thank you, sir, galoshes in green will be fine."

"Here you are, young lady, try that on."

"Yuck."

"We'll take them," said Mary. Because I've got to get out of this store. I just saw a little green creature looking at me. From over in the next aisle.

Gertie pulled Mary into the electronic game aisle, and picked up a Speak and Spell. "Mommy, remember mine?" She held the spelling computer up to Mary. "It's still broken."

E.T.'s mental replicant dove into the computer, and flew through the microchips, rearranging their memory with quick skips of its toes. So when Gertie pressed the Speak and Spell, it said, in E.T.'s voice, *"B. good."*

"Huh?" Gertie stared at it. "Mom, it's, it's—"

"—too expensive," said Mary, and put the Speak and Spell back down on the counter.

"Mom, somebody else might get it, it has a *message* on it!"

"That's right, dear, it says come along with your mother."

"It was E.T.!"

"E.T. is gone, Gertie. Far away."

Just then, Elliott turned the corner in the toy department, with a very odd look on his face. He blinked, dully, toward Mary and Gertie.

"Elliott," said Mary, "what are you doing here? Don't you have a music lesson at this hour?"

Elliott blinked again. "I had the feeling I'd—meet someone here. Someone—"

"Who?" asked Mary.

"He *was* here!" cried Gertie. "Elliott, E.T. was here!"

CHAPTER NINE

The dining hall of the launch base was slowly filling. A starcruiser had returned to the pad, and its pilots were making their way to a table.

The other tables were filling with Micro Techs, whose chairs, of course, were higher. Their manners were deplorable, for they argued fine points of technology and physics while banging their spoons.

When the soup came, they hardly noticed, just spooned it up while they continued arguing—though it was a delicious broth of Bazmat Lizoona. The soup spilled down their chins, and because they dunked their crackers so violently, their fingers needed to be licked continually clean, which they did, in the middle of their bickering.

And then, while brandishing his spoon, one of the Micro Techs started to yawn. His fingers slowly loosened, his spoon fell into his lap, and he collapsed face down in his soup.

A series of little splashes followed, all around the hall, as one Tech after another yawned and fell in the soup. Two moments later the entire dining hall was asleep, under the dominion of the Sleeping Princess, Shemoda Nuncoor, a beautiful veiled spirit of the plant world, spreading her cape over the launch base.

*   *   *

The Flopglopple flopped along beside E.T., and his gaze kept running over E.T.'s form, which was bent, tired, and very, very sad.

40

The Flopglopple reflected: Something's bothering the boss. I should be able to help him.

Instead I have a toe in my ear.

Why?

Because I'm a Flopglopple.

Micron walked beside them, down the canyon path, toward the launch pad. "Don't worry about a thing," he said to E.T. "My logic cells are clicking."

"I'll have not one, but *two* bicycles," said Electrum, "and I shall have them set in a necklace so that I can wear them all the time." The old pirate of the stars laughed heartily, as he'd not done for centuries. Treasure, yes, there'd be much of it—bicycles, paper routes, and Gum.

"And I—" thundered Occulta, "—I shall be a Burger King." He pointed at E.T. "Did not the little Doctor of Greenery describe Burger as the greatest of all things in the universe? Yes, I shall be a Burger King."

The three metallic lords strode fiercely forward, down the canyon path, toward the base. The lights of the base were becoming visible now, through the last ranks of the forest.

"Ah me," sighed E.T. to himself, as he looked down at the launch base. Within it, not a soul stirred, for everyone's face had fallen in his soup, and snores filled the air.

I must be deranged, thought E.T., to have done a thing like this.

But each time he thought of Elliott, growing up a galaxy away with no one to counsel him, he knew he must proceed with his reckless plan. "El-li-ott," he groaned softly.

"Who's this El Li Ott he's always talking about?" asked Sinistro.

"I believe he's a ruler of the fabulous planet Earth," said Electrum. "Thus, he would be one of the Burger Kings."

The dark lords nodded together over this obvious fact, for it would be pointless to cross the universe for anyone less than a potentate of Burger. "He will be rich, of course," said Sinistro. "The Earth word for wealth is moo-la. And we shall have it, my friends, much, much moo-la and—a pogo stick." Sinistro smiled at the ignorance of the others, for he alone had been told about the device. "All the great rulers have a pogo stick. It is kept by their throne for times of emergency. Elliott, the King of Burger, has one in his closet. As you know, we shall each have our own closet."

"Truly, this is a mission worthy of our talents," said Electrum.

"The little doctor has told it all," said Occulta. "Earth's treasures are uncountable. The Monopoly Board, for example, which is worth millions, especially the portion called Boardvark. I must tell you, in advance, Boardvark is mine."

Sinistro cast a sharp glance at his companion but said nothing. However, thought Sinistro, when the time comes, we shall see

who rules Boardvark, from a pogo stick. Wearing the helmet of Foot, and decorated in bicycles.

The launch pad was before them, the great starcruiser at its center.

E.T. put his foot out, and took a step.

"For Elliott."

"Everyone's asleep?" asked the Flopglopple.

"Yes," said E.T.

"Then I'm going to race down."

He ran into the dining hall, where the pilots and the Micro Techs were snoring at their tables. "Asleep in the soup," said the Flopglopple. He lifted up the head of a Micro Tech; noodles were attached to the pugnacious little nose.

E.T. was entering the hall and calling for him.

"Coming," said the Flopglopple, speeding through the aisles.

E.T. looked around at the spectacle of the drugged launch staff, snoring in their bowls. "Wasted," he said to the Flopglopple. "I've wasted the entire crew, and every single technician. I, who'd never hurt a fly, have just rendered two hundred individuals unconscious."

"With their elbows in the salad," said the Flopglopple.

They stepped back outside and joined the other hijackers, who were hurrying toward the ship.

E.T. felt a beam of consciousness from close by, and two old botanists like himself stepped through the hatchway of the ship.

Sinistro's armor plate opened, a long finger extended, and a stream of energy shot from it, forming itself in a magnetic coil around the two botanists and imprisoning them. Repelling their attempts to grip it, it kept them bound to the center of the magnetic field.

The two botanists sat in their whirring magnetic prison, and stared in disbelief at E.T., their minds still unable to comprehend this display of violence. "No one," said one of them softly, "has been forcibly restrained on this planet since—the last beginning, ages ago."

"We board," said Sinistro, pushing past E.T. Electrum and Occulta joined him at the gangplank. They started up the stairs. Suddenly Sinistro was flipped backward through the air, as he had flipped the old botanists, and Electrum and Occulta came tumbling after him.

"The cruiser," said the Flopglopple, "is ringed with a faint glow."

Sinistro was hurling himself against it again, only to be hurled back down the gangplank, his armor plate clattering. Tumbling along the ground, he came to rest at Micron's feet. He looked up, his head and mirror eyes flashing with anger.

"A Repulsor Field. We'll burn our way through."

He raised his laser gun and closed his finger on the trigger. A devastation beam emerged. At the same time the Repulsor Field of the starcruiser converged into a brilliant shield, which, like Sinistro's eyes, reflected all that approached it. The devastation beam was turned back toward Lord Sinistro, and sent him diving for cover. His armor petals flopped over his head and he looked like an umbrella that had been blown inside out.

Electrum put his bullet head down and prepared to ram the ship. A powerful charge gathered in his body and, like some maddened toadstool, he raced up the gangplank. He collided with the Repulsor Field and wavered back and forth, his umbos temporarily flattened and throbbing terribly.

Then, from within the ship came an ominous purring sound, and a gunport opened. A crackling stream of high intensity light shot forth, and like a spinning lariat, encircled Sinistro, Occulta, and Electrum, imprisoning them as they had imprisoned the botanists.

"Let us out! Kill us, but spare us this indignity!" cried Electrum, thumping up and down and rubbing his bruised, misshapen umbos. Sinistro, still resembling a blown-out umbrella, was bending his ribs back into place. And Occulta was slumped on the ground, looking like a cheap, unraveled cigar.

"Come on!" Micron was bouncing around nervously. "Let's get out of here before we're caught!"

E.T. pointed at Sinistro, Occulta, and Electrum. "I can't leave them."

"Why not?"

"Because they will be charged with a crime that is my doing." E.T. sat down with a little *plop*. "I must now go soak my head."

"Where?"

"It is just an expression."

"Well," said Micron, "it seems pointless for me to remain here. I'll be more useful elsewhere. And so—"

He took one quick step, a beam of light shot from the gunport, encircled his foot and held him precisely where he was, as the horizon suddenly filled with ships from the fleet of Lucidulum.

CHAPTER TEN

"You again! What have you to say for yourself this time?"

E.T. looked shamefacedly at the interrogation machine. "I've gone to the dog," he said, from his grab-bag of half-comprehended Earth expressions.

"I beg your pardon?"

"I've been trash-canned. Dumped."

The machine was silent, but its head lights blinked in an erratic pattern, as if a translation was being attempted within. A buzzer sounded, changing the machine's circuit, and its speaker sounded again. "You attempted to steal a grand starship of the fleet of Lucidulum. Why?"

"To see a friend."

"To see a *friend*? Are you mad? A ship of immeasurable power and beauty, equipped for navigation to the ends of time? You take it, to see a friend? As if it were a bus?"

"My friend lives at the end of time." E.T. looked into one of the ocular orbs as it swayed before him. Then the speakers rumbled, spoke again:

"You drugged the entire staff and flight crew of a launch base. Some of them are still in bed. What do you have to say about *that?*"

"Far out."

"Far out? Out where?" The machine spun around, bumped into the wall, spun back again.

"An Earth expression." E.T. twiddled his long toes nervously.

The machine rolled under his nose, sputtering to itself. "You no longer speak the language of the planet, which even I, a programmed machine, can speak. You have changed. What is wrong with you?"

"I'm—I'm—" E.T. struggled. "—a fathead."

The sides of the interrogation machine opened and a calipers came forth; it elongated, measuring E.T.'s brow. "Your head is not fat. It is of the correct size." The calipers were withdrawn and the machine rolled away, hit the wall again, and rolled back. "I repeat—what is wrong with you?"

"I've—flipped my lid."

The machine looked around, orbs twisting. "I see nothing flipped, nor flipping. Answer my question."

"Discombobulated. Lobotomized. Out of it."

The machine started whirring internally, trying to translate. It sputtered again, blew a fuse, and fell silent, motionless, and short circuited.

"Wasted," said E.T., touching it gently.

*   *   *

Botanicus sat in a chair woven of vines and flowers. He shook his head and said, "You cannot steal the fire of the Fleet. Not only is it forbidden, it is impossible."

"What am I to do then?" asked E.T.

"Ponder another solution."

"My solution is far, far away, beyond the Ocean of Lights." E.T. rubbed his brow with his leathery hand. "My head holds many whispers from Earth. My heart holds a feeling. I am bound to Earth, and to Elliott, forever."

Botanicus leaned back in his chair, leaves folding themselves around his head. "My fields hold many secrets."

E.T. withdrew. Outside the chamber of Botanicus were a number of apprentice botanists, youngsters who shied away from E.T. now—for his attempt to borrow a starship was well known.

"Don't pay any attention," said the Flopglopple.

"I shall handle myself with perfect dignity," answered E.T. He elongated his neck to the extreme, until his head was towering; then he put his thumbs in his ears and waved his fingers at the young botanists, who drew back in shock.

"That's wonderful!" cried the Flopglopple, immediately imitating it.

"I learned it from Gertie," said E.T. He continued staring defiantly at the young botanists, and added, "Give me a break."

"Inspired," said the Flopglopple, clapping.

"With practice I'll have every nuance of the language at my command and will be able to fan the breeze like a real numbhead."

"I'm certain of it," nodded the Flopglopple.

"But," said E.T., "if we never get to Earth, what good will my mastery of fanning the breezes do? How will I ever help El-li-ott?"

His voice died on the wind, but his inner feeling went beyond the atmosphere, and crossed the airless gulfs of space, descending to Earth on the high school football field, where it felt a familiar vibration. It was emanating from Elliott's brother, Michael. Tryouts for the varsity team were in progress, and the coach was watching Michael from the sidelines, trying to decide whether or not he was varsity material. He turned to his assistant.

"Whattya think of him?" asked the coach, pointing toward the kicking tee, where Michael was placing the football.

"Naw, he's a washout," said the assistant. "No lift in his kick."

Michael was standing in place now, looking left and right at his teammates as they lined up, awaiting his boot. A few yards ahead of them, E.T.'s telepathic form had found its way to the kicking tee, and had climbed onto the football, for it saw that Michael was very attached to it, and at this very moment considered it the most important object in the world.

"...no *wallop* on his follow-through..."

E.T.'s little telepathic self observed that Michael needed to relax. A beam shot forth from it and hit Michael in the knees, from which it spiraled through his body, adjusting each joint and muscle in a single perfect flex, as Michael brought his arcing foot to the ball.

"...hasn't got any dynamite in his kick..."

KA-BLAMMMMMMMMMM

"Look at that kick! Look!"

The ball was lifting at spaceship velocity and hurtling down field, over the heads of the two waiting receivers, over the goalposts and out over the stone wall surrounding the stadium, where it disappeared from view.

"Put that boy's name on the first team roster."

*   *   *

E.T. and the Flopglopple were walking through the wood above the garden of Botanicus. The path turned, along a natural wall of rock, which was filled with cracks and fissures, one of which had suddenly claimed the attention of the Flopglopple. "Emanation. Mind from the deep!"

E.T. froze with the Flopglopple, and they heard dark voices, echoing in the planet's depths and traveling along through subterranean seams, and exiting from the fissure in front of them.

we never got our bicycles

"Sinistro," said the Flopglopple, and he and E.T. fell to their knees in front of the fissure, and listened to the next transmission:

nor our ballfoot helmets

"Electrum," said E.T. softly.

nor our own closet

"Occulta," concluded the Flopglopple.

The sound of the dark voices grew faint, and traveled on, through other veins.

"Those poor old miners," said E.T. "They were good company, if a little impetuous. And what did they get from me?"

"The shaft," said the Flopglopple.

"I'll make it up to them somehow. After I get myself out of the House of Dogs. For that is what I am in, once again. But do you know something?"

"What?"

"I don't give a fudge."

He led the way into a far garden, where row after row of tall, simple-looking plants grew. But no sooner had he started down the first row, than one of the green stalks swung out, forcing him to his knees.

Duck or be struck, said a soft vegetal voice.

"B. good," said E.T.

But one of the branches crept beneath him, grabbed him by the leg and lifted him in the air. He hung there, upside-down.

The Flopglopple addressed the plant: "Antum Tadana, this is why no one wishes to attend to your needs."

Antum Tadana shook E.T. in the air by one foot. E.T. groaned to the Flopglopple. "Don't antagonize him. Flatter him. That is how you handle Antum Tadana."

The Flopglopple nodded, and moved closer to the tall plant. "Antum Tadana, give me five seconds to turn on all your nutrient valves, for you are the true source of all inspiration, here, there, and everywhere. The only good idea anyone ever had came from you. You are the wisest, most vigorous and charming of all plants in the universe."

I like that kind of talk, said Antum Tadana.

His long branches lowered, the tendrils opened, and the plant set E.T. back on the ground.

E.T. joined the Flopglopple, opening the nutrient valves, and whispering quietly, "If the truth be told, Antum Tadana is one of the ingredients used in breakfast cereal."

"I see," said the Flopglopple.

"He must never know," said E.T., and crept to the next row, mumbling praise and flattery, and Antum Tadana watched, branches folded, basking in the sound of praise of his most high and mighty self, never dreaming he was Tum Tad's Crunch Flakes.

They continued on, to the garden of Magdol, the Sulking Beauty. "Her flowers are the most prized in the capitals," said E.T., "but she's a plant who likes to be coaxed."

"How do we do that?"

"We sing to her," said E.T. And he began to croak in his rasping voice, an ancient lullaby of the planet.

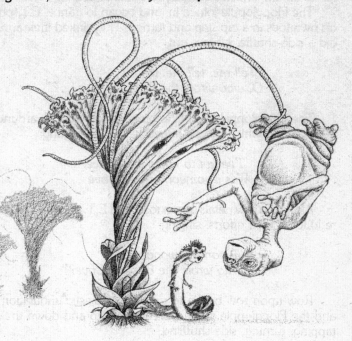

> *"Opis nazbeth, shipta-ba'lu*
> *Urumolk, opi majo vashnu..."*

The central plant in the row lifted one of her stalks very slowly. *I'm tired of that old junk,* said the Sulking Beauty.

"Her petals are drooping," said the Flopglopple. "She wants a new song."

E.T. pondered, hands clasped behind his back. A new song, a new song...

He turned, put out his arms and sang:

> *"Going to Kamsas City*
> *Kamsas City, here I come..."*

and snatches of everything else he'd heard on Elliott's Fabulous Fifties album, which he'd played in the closet.

The Flopglopple joined in, and began to dance. E.T. pointed his own toes in a tap step and turned. They linked their arms and did a side-shuffle, elbows out.

> *"Tell me, tell me, tell me,*
> *O, who wrote the Book of Love...?"*

The Flopglopple spun like a top, raising dust all around him in a dancing whirl, and he joined E.T. as they sang:

> *"I've got to know the answer*
> *Was it someone from above..."*

Along the row petals began to lift and E.T. and the Flopglopple redoubled their efforts, singing:

> *"I wonder, wonder who*
> *Who wrote the Book of Love?"*

Row upon row began to unfold in majestic undulation. E.T. and the Flopglopple panted and puffed up and down the rows, tapping, turning, side-shuffling.

"A-bop-bop-a-loom-op
A-lop bop boom!
Tutti Frutti au rutti..."

Magdol's garden opened, and E.T. and the Flopglopple kept dancing to keep her open and lure her along.

"I've been to the east
I've been to the west
but she's the gal I love the best
Tutti Frutti au rutti..."

The Flopglopple was in ecstasy, for dancing and jumping around were his most cherished pastimes, and to be doing it with his friend, for a good cause, made it a most unusual occurrence, for usually when he was jumping and dancing he got yelled at for breaking something. But this! This was official! He and E.T. spun about, arms outstretched, singing:

"Deep down in Lou'siana, close to New
    Orleans,
'Way back up in the woods among the
    evergreens,
There stood an old log cabin made of earth and
    wood,
Where lived a country boy named Johnny
    B. GOODE."

CHAPTER ELEVEN

Long shadows were falling. E.T. and the Flopglopple were sitting on craggly old meteorite pieces buried in the ground a billion years ago. The rays of the sun, called Monshoo, Gigantic Blossom, were shining their last splendid colors of the day. E.T.'s heart-light answered, shining its own ruby rays back at Monshoo as it descended, closing itself within the leaves of evening.

"The others show their hearts too," said the Flopglopple. In the distance, on the surrounding hilltops, more heart-lights were going on, as all the botanists paused to answer the great blossom of the dying sun.

Then it was gone below the horizon, and E.T. gazed at the illusions left in the clouds—of a mountain range. Its peaks and slopes were calling him. But why?

He called to the cloud, as if to hear an echo or an answer. "El-li-ott!"

"LL-EE-UT," said a voice from the shadows.

A robot glided forward, his belly rockets firing gently. The Flopglopple's neck shot forward to within a hair of the iron head. "An old model."

"Yes," said the robot in a clicking voice. "I'm old. But I'm spry."

Four mechanical legs creaked down out of his frame and touched ground, supporting him. He shook one of them off to the side in a little dance step, to show his nimbleness, then shut his hover rockets off. His metal tentacles were covered with rust and his joints were squeaking.

"Officially scrapped," he said. "But I have hundreds of years of experience. I analyze and synthesize. And I'm searching—"

He paused, his electric eyes blinking slowly. "—for the truth."

He gestured toward them with one of his metal tentacles. "Can you help me?"

"We can oil your joints," said E.T.

"Most kind of you. Haven't had oiling in ages." The robot looked at his chest. "Could do with some rust-proof paint, as well."

* * *

"Well, well," said Micron, "a vintage model."

"I'm old, but I'm nimble," said the robot, and leapt in the air, attempting to click his heels.

"Bizarre behavior," said Micron. "Needs his board checked." He turned the robot around. "Snap open, please."

"Certainly," said the robot, and his back panel opened.

Micron went inside, his skilled fingers racing over the robot's mind banks. "Hmmmmm, yes, one of the old navigator attendants, isn't that right?"

"Yes," said the robot, "I have logged six trillion, one billion, five million, six-hundred thousand, four-hundred and twenty-three and two-tenths miles."

E.T. stepped closer. "You know how to fly?"

*   *   *

In an innermost chamber of the capital of Lucidulum, whose location and description cannot yet be revealed, a report was made by the Contentment Monitor to one who must be nameless.

"The Doctor of Botany, formerly First Class, now demoted, has gone about his new assignment with enthusiasm."

"No more talk of starships?"

"None. He is, in fact, engaged in independent hybrid experiments, wholly contained to the fields of Botanicus."

"What are these experiments?"

"Simple cross-pollenizations. He seems happy." The Contentment eye blinked. "He has befriended an old robot, who has become devoted to him. The robot is a model we scrapped long ago, and ordinarily we would simply dismantle it, but since the Doctor of Botany has suffered from intense loneliness, my section recommends he be allowed to keep the robot."

"What is the robot's program?"

"I inquired directly of the robot. It said it was searching for truth." The CM's eye crinkled with a smile. "An obvious malfunction, but completely harmless."

"Very well. Your recommendation may stand."

*   *   *

The greenhouse had been swept out by the Flopglopple, and its glass had been cleaned by the robot.

"This plant," said the robot, "he is special?"

"Antum Tadana contains the seed of a great energy," said the Flopglopple.

The robot moved on to a homely little plant, within which a modest vegetable was beginning to appear. "And this?"

"It is called a turnip," said E.T., "and this is what we are going to do with it—"

The little turnip sat, mutely brooding on the new activity bred into it; strange un-turnip-like surges were suffusing it, and its outer shell was growing harder than any turnip's ever had before.

The robot hummed mechanically as he weeded and watered the Fusion Bloom plant. "Don't touch," said the robot, when the Flopglopple came near. A muffled roar was heard, and the tenacious roots of the plant had to grip hard to keep it in place, as plasma exhaust came out the back end of the little fruit, along with a single floating seed. "It has dined," said the robot, and moved to the next one, where the process was repeated.

"A most energetic little plant," said the Flopglopple, as the muffled roar was repeated all down the row.

As for the turnip, it couldn't help wondering inside itself at the odd sensations permeating its cells. If it could have spoken it would have said that it was some turnip indeed.

And then its leaves suddenly turned up at the ends, and its roots began to tingle.

Botanicus entered the greenhouse.

"A new experiment, Doctor?"

"For a bigger—turnip."

Botanicus stepped over to the pot where the little vegetable was growing. He stroked its surface gently.

E.T. knew that in the next moment the order would come to dismantle everything. Would a reprimand follow as well? More time in the House of Dogs?

"I strongly recommend," said Botanicus, pointing to the turnip, "that you include the nutrients Lota-120 and Ertong Number 7." He stroked its leaves. "They will add intelligence and elasticity to the walls. And you will want that."

*   *   *

"Contentment Monitor approaching," said the robot. "On local Course Zero Two Six, south by southeast..."

The Contentment Monitor streaked down to E.T.'s greenhouse.

"You seem happy, Doctor."

E.T. bent over his turnip, which had now doubled in size. "All is going well."

"A new food, is it?"

"Bred for harsh conditions," said E.T.

"Very good," said the Contentment Monitor. It spun over to the robot. "And you, Mechanical Object, are you content?"

The robot's electronic brain clicked and beeped as it bent over the Fusion Blooms. "I search for truth."

Permanent malfunction, noted the Contentment Monitor. *But it's harmless.*

And the Monitor sped away.

E.T. smiled to himself, and a thought-wave went out through his telepathic portal.

The robot saw it go, and quickly calculated its course. "Outer Range Five Zero Five, Gate of Immensity, destination—Earth."

* * *

Gertie, carrying a box of soap powder, walked with her mother toward the door of the Laundromat.

Mary heaved through the door and flopped the basket down in front of the coin-operated machines. "Did you bring the change, honey?"

"Elliott took it all to play Space Invaders."

Mary sighed, took a dollar bill out of her purse and went to the change-making machine. It swallowed her dollar, chewed it thoughtfully, and spit it back out as unsuitable.

. . . course five zero five, destination Earth . . .

E.T.'s telepathic beam, homing in on Mary's vibration, entered through the roof of the Laundromat and landed in a dryer, where it was spun around at a high speed.

Gertie, sitting in the laundry basket, looked up. A row of tropical plants hung in the window, and every one of them had just blossomed, petals opening out in a riotous burst of color.

"E.T.!"

E.T.'s beam shot into the change machine, analyzed its mechanism and tripped it until the thing emptied itself, spilling quarters all over the floor.

"Shhhhhh," said Mary to Gertie, as they quickly scooped up the jackpot.

CHAPTER TWELVE

E.T. walked along until he found the Jumpum Elder, surrounded by little Jumpums who were watching him bounce. As if on a trampoline, he sailed into the air, branches waving. He came down lightly, his canopy of silken leaves and branches acting like a parachute.

As he landed, he perceived E.T.'s presence, and leapt to E.T.'s side. *Jumping Time!*

"Elder Jumpum," said E.T., "I will jump with you, but I need a favor."

Anyone who jumps around with me has only to ask, said the Elder, and he leaned down to listen to E.T.'s request.

* * *

"Increasing in size at an alarming rate," said the robot, his calipers telescoped to their full length around the giant turnip.

"It's as big as the greenhouse that once held it," said the Flopglopple proudly, for the plant was thriving marvelously in the outdoor spot he'd chosen for it.

"Contentment Monitor approaching," said the robot. E.T. signaled with his heart-light, into the forest.

The Elder Jumpum saw the light and called to his family. *Jump to it!*

They bounced out of the forest toward the greenhouse-sized turnip. The bigger Jumpums surrounded it, and the little Jumpums leapt up and clung to its sides. And the Elder Jumpum took a flying leap to the very top of it, as the Contentment Monitor paused overhead and looked down:

59

"Jumpums jumping for joy. Very contented. Probably holding a jumping contest." It sped off to file its Well-being Report.

*   *   *

"Truly," said the robot, "this is one of the great vegetables."

"Inject Lota 120," said E.T. The turnip, enormous now, and realizing it was like no other turnip ever created, drank deeply of the growth accelerator; it knew itself to be indestructible, with skin and roots akin to stone and steel, but it could not surmise its destiny. *I'm one tough turnip,* it reflected to itself, and let it go at that.

* * *

"Look who's coming, Elliott," said Michael.

Elliott looked down the hall of the crowded mall, and felt a strange sensation pass over him as *she* came into view, her pony-tail swinging. "So what," he said, jamming his hands in his pockets.

"Elliott's got a gur-ul friend," sang Gertie.

"She's just somebody in my class," said Elliott, his legs turning to soft ice cream as she passed and gave him a sly little smile and a little toss of her ponytail. He pivoted like a windup toy, as she walked on down the hall.

At that moment, one of E.T.'s little replicant beams came down through the roof of the mall and bonked Elliott right on the conk, and bounced off without touching a single communication nerve—for Elliott was standing still as a statue, staring after the ponytail.

*   *   *

In the shadows outside the Micro Tech base, Micron struck a single note on his a'lud. A moment later a cloaked individual joined him in the shadows. "You brought it?" asked Micron.

"You'll find it in a service vehicle parked in the hills."

"A complete command console?"

"More or less. You'll have to improvise on a few things, but it's a functional system."

"And where did it come from?"

"That is for me alone to know," said the other, who despite his cloak of hiding could only be another Micro Tech. "They will learn in Lucidulum not to demote fellows like me." And with these words he moved quickly off.

Micron found the old service vehicle, as promised, climbed in and fired up the engine. Congratulating himself on his cleverness in obtaining it, he lifted the service vehicle aloft and flew away.

"Follow him," said the Micro guard, and a launch security ship entered the air a short distance away.

Micron, flying without lights, sailed over the vast agricultural realm. "I'm a clever sort. I move silently and leave no tracks."

"I'm locked with him, sir," said the pilot of the security ship.

"Good," said the Micro commander. "I wonder where the idiot thinks he's going?"

"...making no waves, not a ripple..." Micron touched his controls and banked left. It was then he noticed twin lights following his trackless track.

"Uh-oh." He flipped the aft-scanner on and saw his pursuers dipping with him over the trees. He increased his speed and prayed the old service vehicle wouldn't fly apart at the seams.

His pursuers dove with him and closed. "We can lock him to our hull in a moment, sir."

"Proceed."

Micron shot from the valley, planing again over the great black forest, moonlight glinting on his swept wingtips.

His automatic navigator clicked on, code-stimulated from the ground, by one who now guided Micron's ship.

"Course two five evader should do nicely," said the robot, who stood in the forest in a narrow lane of trees, wide enough for one service vehicle. An electronic beam fired out of his forehead, up the black lane of trees toward the nose of Micron's ship.

Micron felt his landing gear click down, heard number one and two aft engines shut off, and the docking and orientation thrusters firing on as the service vehicle dropped down into the trees.

The pursuit ship tried to drop with it. "Impossible," said the pilot, "I've no room." The forest lane seemed to be dancing, trees hopping about. The entire forest below had changed shape, the forest lane gone, the trees densely grouped. He looked at his commander and shook his head. "We've lost him."

*   *   *

"The sky is clear now," said Micron to E.T. "I've got to get this SV out of here and ditch it."

The equipment he'd brought had been unloaded. E.T. signaled the Jumpums, and a runway opened up again in the forest, trees dancing apart. Their crimes had multiplied again. He'd stolen classified equipment and—

He looked at the dancing trees, who, immediately after Micron's takeoff were forming close knit camouflage once more.

—he'd corrupted the Jumpums.

*   *   *

The Flopglopple and the robot worked with him, grafting the Fusion Blooms to the circumference of the giant turnip; the tough tendrils of the Fusion were soon circling the turnip, clinging to its surface.

The robot gazed at it, his head clicking audibly. "I don't understand, for now it will be all the more difficult to extract the edible center. However, vegetables are not my field."

CHAPTER THIRTEEN

An agi Jabi plant appeared on the hilltop, frantically waving its scarecrow arms and giving the warning to E.T.'s camp.

Monitors approaching, southwest, V-formation, considerable numbers.

E.T. and Flopglopple waved to their family of Jumpums, who twisted their roots around the turnip in an unbreakable grip.

"Monitors entering our area," said the robot, "south by southwest."

The whirling orbs, like a flight of little cyclones, flashed over the horizon. "This is the demoted doctor's sector," said the point Monitor. "Look sharply."

"Now," said E.T. to the Jumpums. All around the turnip, the attached Jumpums curled their powerful root systems; then they seemed to crouch a little, and then they jumped.

The turnip broke free of the ground, the great vegetable sailing into the air, carried by the Jumpums.

This is jumping, said the Jumpums, bearing the turnip lightly between them, on a long gliding leap that carried them out over a nearby lake. They floated down, leaves fluttering, and sank beneath its surface.

Immersion, reflected the turnip. *My fate is a mixed one. But I am patient, for something great awaits me.*

When the Monitors landed, E.T. was puttering in an experimental garden he'd created, his robot beside him. The Monitors circled the robot. "Old Machine, what has been going on here?"

The robot's head beeped and whirred. "Gardening detail... briiiick... I trim and clip... as instructed."

"I don't believe him," said one of the Monitors. "Open up
your panel."

The robot obeyed, and the Monitor darted inside the robot's
back, activating his immediate memory. "And now—give me a
readout, Old Machine."

E.T. groaned to himself, for the robot's readout would tell all.

A length of paper was ejected from the robot's mouth, and
E.T. groaned again, as the Monitors gathered around it, reading.

"Hmmmmm," said the leader. "Well, it is just as he said.
Simple gardening, cutting and planting. Since the machine cannot
speak falsely—" The Monitors whirled off as quickly as they'd
come, and E.T. looked at the robot.

"A faulty wire," said the robot, raising one finger. "Very handy
sometimes when one is questioned."

*   *   *

The Jumpums emerged in a fountainous burst from the lake,
and brought the giant turnip down on the shore among the huge
boulders which it so closely resembled.

"You are good friends," said E.T.

Just some good-natured jumping, said the Jumpums, and
jumped off, back toward the forest.

From around the edge of the lake, a large lizard approached,
and behind it, the figure of Botanicus.

"Watering your turnip, Doctor?" Botanicus slowly circled the
giant plant. He touched the edges of the Fusion Blooms that
covered the skin, and examined their pulsating petals. "There is
a plant," he said, still musing, "whose rhizome is pure lightning."
He looked at E.T. "Great skill is needed in handling it, for it holds
the last vibration of eternity, that force which thrilled the Cosmic
Egg in the beginning. I speak of Dagon Sabad, the mountain
reed."

*   *   *

The mountain trail was steep and E.T.'s legs were short. More-
over, the region of the mountain was untamed, and it was here
that the strangest plants of all were known to grow. Even on the

lower slopes, the species known as Nistus Opa, the Illusionist, was at work—from its petals a faint wraith flowing. E.T. looked, and saw Elliott, shaped in mist, waving to him.

"El-li-ott!"

"An illusion," said the Flopglopple, reminding him and tugging him on by. "It reads your dreams and answers them."

The robot had stopped, and was staring into the flower-mist, where he saw an image of a vintage model robot like himself, with opposite polarity, a charming machine, very delicate and winking at him. "... briiick... briiiiz... how do you do," he answered, attempting to kiss its misty hand.

"Come on," said the Flopglopple, tapping the robot on the head with a soft clunk. The robot blinked and looked away from the mist. "A dream?"

"A dream," said the Flopglopple.

"We robots rarely dream, except for short bursts of static. I must say—" He kept turning back as the Flopglopple dragged him on. "—it is a most pleasant activity."

"El-li-ott... El-li—ott..."

The Flopglopple ran back and grabbed E.T. again, prodding him away from the illusion and on up the path.

I alone, reflected the Flopglopple, *am not susceptible to Nistus Opa, for my dreams are hidden, even from myself.*

The trail led out of the brush, and narrowed, with rock on one side and a sheer drop on the other. E.T. looked down into the chasm, its bottom lost in shadows. The trail turned a corner in the cliff, and they edged around it.

bounce bounce bounce

They heard it, then saw it—a mountain Jumpum, very light and springy, wildly bouncing toward them on the narrow path, roots up, branches flying.

boing boing boing

It hogged the path, seeing nothing, enjoying itself. Its roots curled under and it sprang straight at them. E.T. dove into the dirt.

The Flopglopple and the robot fell with him, and the mountain Jumpum sailed over them.

"... briiick..."

"... oh no..."

"...hold tight..."

Sounded like voices back there, thought the mountain Jumpum as it continued down the path. *Must be hearing things.*

bounce bounce bounce

E.T.'s party brushed itself off, and continued cautiously along the path. But now the day was ending, and long shadows were falling upon the mountain. And within the shadows were other shadows, of the Fearful Potencies, shape-shifting in black. "They are the Urumolki," said E.T. "They cannot be tamed."

One wrapped itself around E.T. and turned him gently back toward the cliff, as if to lead him over it. Another wrapped itself around the Flopglopple, and spun him toward the cliff, for the Urumolki do not like visitors on their mountain.

"Buzzzz...cliiiick...beep...that will be quite enough, thank you." The robot's powerful arms reached out to E.T. and the Flopglopple, stripping them of their shadows and snapping the black forms like an old tablecloth. The Urumolki collapsed, into black shapes no bigger than a sparrow's wings. The robot tossed them away in the air, and they vanished in flight. "Must have thought we were cold and needed shawls...cricck...beep... considerate of them, but...buzzzz...cumbersome things, could trip someone."

"Thank you," said E.T. "We were almost—ding swizzled."

*   *   *

Night enveloped the mountain. They walked by the light of the robot's eyes, which sent bright twin beams out, through the darkness. His head turned here and there, sweeping the area in front of them. The Flopglopple flopped along beside E.T. "Where does this plant we search for dwell?"

"I don't know," said E.T. "I don't even know what Dagon Sabad looks like. All the texts say is that it must be found at night, for its power to be full."

Their climb had brought them to a smooth plateau, where the Near Moon shone. The robot's eye beams penetrated the plateau, and caught movement. A shadow swept out, gigantic, and rose up—a black cape that cloaked the moon. "Urumolki!" cried E.T.

"Extending hospitality again . . . cliiiiick."

"Run!" cried the Flopglopple.

E.T.'s tongue was tied in fright, but his Earth language finally unloosened, with "Beat it!"

"Very well," said the robot, and ejected a wire rugbeater from the end of his arm. "Beating as directed . . . crackle beep . . ."

The menacing shadow snapped in the air, struck like a rug on a clothes line by the robot. "Swift strokes to get the dust out . . . bricccckle . . . breep." The Urumolki fell to the ground, flattened.

"A picnic cloth . . . bleeep . . . apparently that was the intention, to make a nice place on the ground for us. Pity we have no food and a thermos of lubricating oil."

*   *   *

The peak of the mountain was broad, and E.T. felt the power of Dagon Sabad sending out its current, unlike anything he'd ever experienced before.

The robot's arms were angled out, receiving the energy flow and computing it inwardly, a length of tape shooting like a serpent's tongue from his chin slot and flapping in the wind. "High molecular activity . . . beep . . ."

Lightning flashed, illuminating the dark clouds and the mountaintop, rock ledges momentarily flooded with a ghostly hue.

The Flopglopple rolled around, vertebrae snapping ecstatically, as if manipulated by four-hundred electric hands.

The robot's eye beams began a stroboscopic pulsing, intensely bright. ". . . briiiickitttaaa . . . rrrrrrttt . . . increasing voltage, becoming immeasurable."

Flaps opened on both sides of the robot's head and four glowing rods shot out, and electricity began jumping from rod to rod around his head. ". . . rrrrrrkkkkkk . . . zzzzzzzz . . . charging batteries . . . dee—licious."

The Flopglopple snapped along over the ground, a limp lightning-charged noodle, his snaps carrying him to the unseen edge of the cliff, off which he suddenly found himself hanging by two fingers. He hung happily, singing to himself.

E.T. continued his shuffling step. "Dagon Sabad, ruler of all plants, possibly greater than even Antum Tadana—"

Possibly greater?

Lightning splintered the dark, momentarily sizzling the shadowy tip of a small and nearly invisible shoot of vegetation. And then lightning seemed to be drawn down, swallowed in the shoot itself.

Antum Tadana would perish here, in a little pile of burnt breakfast flakes.

The robot stood beside E.T., eye beams pointed toward the lightning-charged reed; his head was wreathed as if with sparklers. "...criiickit...reeeeep...planetary power source. Directly ahead. Incalculable emission...beyond outmoded computer's power to analyze."

E.T. took a step forward, and felt his toes suddenly freeze, imprisoned in place by a magnetic force rising up through the stones, and the robot froze beside him. "...malfunction in my extremities. Ground grippers locked in the joints. Oiling recommended."

The Flopglopple pulled himself up by his finger and rushed across the mountaintop toward E.T. and the robot, only to find his feet suddenly glued in place and the rest of his body elongating forward and then snapping back like a rubber band.

Thus the exploration party stood, fastened in the stones before the altar of Dagon Sabad, and E.T. knew this power gripping them could hold them for days, nights, weeks, ages.

"I—seek a cutting from your shoot."

Certainly, certainly, said the plant, but E.T. sensed that nothing now was certain.

E.T. reached down to it, and his healing finger glowed, for he must anesthetize the plant first; then with tender care, he broke it off.

A sheet of fire sprang out of it, rising like a geyser, high above the mountain peak. He was knocked backward with the roar, as a fountain of radiance lit the sky, flowing from the mouth of a plant no bigger than E.T.'s little finger. He whispered his thanks to the mother reed and slowly backed away, the cutting clutched in his hand.

"Stellar magma...blip..." The robot was pointing to the blazing spectacle overhead.

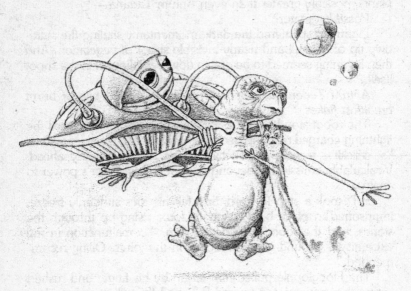

"Come on," said E.T., "let's beat it."

The robot's rugbeater came out.

"No," said E.T., "I mean, we must leave."

As he backed away, his eyes met another surge of light. Intermediate cruisers had blasted off, and were streaking toward the mountain, for its eruption had illuminated the night sky in all directions.

"Hurry," said E.T., though his legs were shortest and slowest, rocking in little steps across the mountaintop. The Flopglopple and the robot lifted him between them, and hauled him quickly along over the plateau. "Beep beep...maximum acceleration," said the robot.

They sped across the rough peak and dove down a rocky incline as the cruisers of Lucidulum shot by.

"Owch, owch, owch." E.T. tumbled along between the robot and the Flopglopple as the mountainside was suddenly lit with enormous search beams from the cruisers. The robot hurried forward, down the narrow ledge, E.T. and the Flopglopple following.

bounce bounce bounce

"Look," said the robot, turning the other way, and pointing, to where the mountain Jumpum was bouncing—a right angle bounce, into a crevice in the cliffside, where it disappeared.

E.T., the robot, and the Flopglopple scrambled after the Jumpum, through a huge fissure in the rock. They heard the Jumpum's bounces echoing down, down, down.

bou-ounce bou-ounce bou-ounce

The robot's bright eye beams clicked on, down a long jagged tunnel in the mountain.

CHAPTER FOURTEEN

"Nobody's home, are they?" asked Elliott in a fearful whisper.

"No," said Julie, "they're gone."

The house belonged to the Zontack family, and Mr. Zontack was well-known for throwing babysitters' boyfriends out through the side door with a foot implanted in their designer jeans.

"Want to watch TV?" asked Julie.

"Naw, we should keep it quiet, right? So we can hear somebody drive up?"

"You *are* afraid of Mr. Zontack."

"Well, he hung Tyler out a window upside-down."

"That's because Tyler's a creep."

"He was helping to babysit."

"He was raiding the refrigerator."

"I won't go near it," said Elliott, quickly. He looked around the living room. On the wall was a picture of Mr. Zontack, with a large shark hanging beside him at the end of a pier. Mr. Zontack appeared to have punched it to death.

Elliott opened the curtain and saw a flickering red light over the houses. It was sailing around confusedly, up and down the block, and then crash-dived into a dish antenna in somebody's yard. Elliott opened the door and ran outside. "E.T.!" he shouted. "E.T.!"

But the light had died out with a little hissing sound, and now the street was silent.

Except for the sound of an approaching automobile.

Elliott leapt into the darkness between the houses and pressed himself against the side of the building. The car slowed, and pulled to a stop, and Mr. Zontack got out.

"Somebody's been here."

"Would you please calm down?" said his wife.

"I can always tell when some young punk comes around. Eating everything in the refrigerator. Snooping."

Elliott slipped onto his bike and rolled it out of the backyard. He pushed it past a few houses, then brought it back up through the yards, onto the street, right in front of the dish antenna. "Thank you, E.T.," he said softly, and rode away.

*   *   *

Botanicus peered out of the cave door. "A great many Security ships up there," he said, nodding to the sky, where the search for E.T. continued. Botanicus patted the side of the vine-covered turnip at the mouth of the cave. "But you're well hidden. So—" He turned back to E.T. "I shall leave you to your work."

E.T. stepped with him to the mouth of the cave. "Why have you helped me?"

"A culture such as ours, whose evolution is complete, needs a shock now and then. How shall I put it—it needs—"

"—a bug in its ear?"

"Yes, that's it. Exactly. It needs a bug in its ear." Botanicus walked out into the open. Very handy, these Earth expressions.

*   *   *

The robot went to a nearby Jumpum tree. "Lift up, please." The Jumpum lifted a long root, revealing the hiding place of a number of high intensity tools. "Thank you." The robot carried a laser torch back to the cave. He pointed it at the turnip. "Kitchen duty. Preparing vegetable."

The thick toughened skin slowly yielded and a door-shaped wedge was cut out of the turnip's face. The robot's metal fingers retracted and were replaced by a pair of pointed digging tools. "Emergency service items. Entrenchment orders, briizz."

And he hollowed out the turnip.

*   *   *

E.T. turned to his Flopglopple, who was dancing with his shadow in the back of the cave, where a few Lumens burned for him. "Turn and step...one two..." The Flopglopple reached out, actually embraced and gripped his shadow, hand to hand, as E.T. watched in amazement.

"Flopglopple, you are astounding."

The shadow melted from the Flopglopple's grip, as he seemed to wake in his dancing from some deep spell. "Did you—did you speak?"

"Gather the Rakoor Ram, vine of pliable grace. We can shape it here, strengthen it with Antum Tadana, and bend it to our needs."

The Flopglopple drew back one leg, poising himself for a streaking dash. A final word from E.T. cautioned him:

"Many search the mountains, hills, and forest for us now. Do not be captured."

"A Flopglopple is not easily overtaken," said the creature, and sped off, out into the night.

E.T. stepped from the door of the turnip and walked wearily to the rear of the cave, where he had grown a little fungus bed for himself, and onto which he laid himself with a sigh. "A Flopglopple is not easily overtaken, but a dry old demoted Doctor of Botany, formerly First Class, may not be so difficult a quarry." He sighed again and rolled over. In very little time, exhausted from his labors and his constant hiding, he fell asleep.

His thought-wave switched to the telepathic frequency, and his tele-replicant went out through the mountain cave, and into the universal spaces. It crossed the Pass to Immensity and, piercing the dimensions, came down on Earth in Elliott's house, where only Harvey the dog was at home, chewing on an old baseball glove.

Not much flavor left in this. I'm in desperate need of a Milk-Bone.

He wandered into the kitchen.

They always make these shelves too high for the average dog.

His paws were up on the counter, his snout straining, but he couldn't reach the box of Milk-Bones, which was plainly visible and precariously balanced.

If we had a canary, I could train him to fly up there.

Harvey lowered his paws, just as E.T.'s little replicant shot in and bounced around from wall to wall.

A little more to the left, said Harvey, directing the bounce.

The replicant landed on the Milk-Bone box, with just enough weight to tip it over, spilling the contents on the floor in the sort of disordered pile appealing to dogs.

Thank you, said Harvey, wading into it, jaws open.

The little E.T. form expired in the cupboard.

* * *

The Flopglopple stalked through the woods, with loops of Rakoor Ram over his shoulder; his step was alternately cautious and carefree, according to his nature. "I trust to speed," he said to himself, as he gathered more of the strong pliable vine.

But the forest was filled with Micro Techs, riding in little two-seater pods, very fast and maneuverable.

"They seem upset about something," remarked the Flopglopple to himself, not knowing that Micro Techs cannot bear to have something of theirs lost, misplaced, unaccounted for, or otherwise out-of-line. That an entire command console, four life-support systems, and an atomic clock had vanished made their big round eyes pop from their heads.

The Flopglopple waved to them.

He wondered why.

Probably, he thought, speeding off in a blur, because I'm a Flopglopple.

The drivers of the pods were shifting gears, pods streaking into high. But then, throughout the woods, it suddenly became—

Jumping time!

The forest began to move, trees leaping every which way, forming chutes, cul-de-sacs, circles, parades, chorus lines, and spinning wheels. Pods crashed into rocks, into lakes, into each other, and the Flopglopple sped over several hillsides in the meantime, still clutching his loops of Rakoor Ram, the vine of grace.

With disappointment he looked back down the hillside at the Micro Techs, who were out of the chase and swearing at each other, blaming each other for the collisions.

"They're fast," remarked the Flopglopple, "but not fast

enough." He zoomed away, and very shortly had brought the vines of pliable grace to E.T.

"Did you have any trouble?"

"None," said the Flopglopple.

*   *   *

The Rakoor Ram vine was taken into the turnip and shaped into a sphere of interlocking points, nearly as big as the turnip shell itself.

"Now," said E.T., "we must fix Dagon Sabad at each of these twists." He indicated the spots where they'd intertwined the vine into little cups, and into each of these cups a shoot of Dagon Sabad was placed.

"A lovely garden," said the robot, nodding at the spherical arbor. "A perfect decoration you have made in secret, briiiiick cliiiiiick, and we will present it to the Lords of Lucidulum. Is this your plan?"

"Something like that," said E.T.

*   *   *

"It's working perfectly," said Elliott to Michael, as they walked through the school hallway. "I've been playing hard-to-get and Julie's nuts about me."

"Well," said Michael, "don't out-cool yourself."

"Mike, I know what I'm doing. I understand the *moves*."

"Here's my class," said Michael, turning into a doorway. "See you later."

Elliott turned the corner of the hall and saw Julie standing there, talking to Snork Johnson, captain of the junior swimming team, who could swim underwater from here to Japan.

Elliott wanted to step between them and drill Snork Johnson between the eyes. After which Snork Johnson would beat him senseless.

Julie, can't you see I'm standing here?

She did not see him standing there, or if she did, she didn't seem to care.

Julie, sighed Elliott, oh Julie.

CHAPTER FIFTEEN

In the innermost chamber of Lucidulum, the Contentment Monitor made his report. "My unit investigated the demoted Doctor of Botany."

"And?"

"Though all seemed to be in order, I was not satisfied. I went, therefore, to inquire of Botanicus, chief of the agricultural sector."

"And what did Master Botanicus say?"

"He said the doctor was working on a bug. Apparently one that troubles the ear."

"Good, he is finally doing useful work."

"Yes, sir."

* * *

"A dozen ruined pods!" shouted the head of Micro Tech Security. "I send you out to find valuable stolen equipment and you ruin what equipment we own. Junk!" He pointed at the dented, wrinkled, racked-up pods, which now lay in a heap outside Micro Tech Headquarters. The head of Security was hopping about in fury, his eyes bulging, his transparent interior a tornado of temper. "Nincompoops! Imbeciles!"

"Sir, the forest kept jumping around."

"An entire forest jumping around?" screamed the head of Security as he jumped around. "Do you expect me to believe that?"

"Sir—"

"Shut up. Repair those pods! And resume your search!"

* * *

E.T. entered his own village again, and made his way toward the family gourd.

"Hello, my Parent," he said, stepping along the little garden path.

"Welcome, child. You have been away at your new green-house?"

"Yes," said E.T. "I've created a very large turnip."

"And your ger-a-ni-um? Is that how it is called?"

"Yes, my Gertie geranium. I have caused it to flourish."

"Good," said the Parent. "The blossoms of the universe should be spread. It is the truest diplomacy, for *our soul is in the flower,* as the old writings have it."

"You have taught me all," said E.T. "And I must apply your teachings." He bent to a tiny patch of emerald herbs and min-istered to them as he spoke. "I won't see you again for a while. My new researches shall claim all my attention, night and day."

The Parent looked at him, eyes holding a strange glitter.

*   *   *

In the night, then, when the gourd was still and even the Lumens were sleeping, E.T. rose from his bed and walked softly down the neck of the gourd toward the Parent's chamber. He held a single Lumen by a thread, the sleepy Lumen's light flick-ering on and off as it dreamed.

E.T. entered the chamber. There, stretched out on its own bed, was the Parent, ages old.

He bent over the beloved sleeping form, and touched his finger lightly to the Parent's forehead and whispered, *"I'll be right here."*

*   *   *

A semicircle of computerized units—the assembled command module—wrapped itself around Micron and the robot, who sat before the many controls, pressing buttons. "Give me fore ... aft ... trim," said Micron.

"Number One firing," said the robot, as the Fusion Bloom

roared, plasma streaming through the wall of the turnip, into the outside air.

"Good," said Micron. "Let's try the entire lower ring."

The lower ring of Fusion Blooms roared, in a sound that vibrated the floor of the turnip under E.T.'s feet.

Outside, the lizards watched, as the turnip's lower portion was lit in a net of glowing plasma.

"Close main valves," said Micron to the robot. "We don't want to draw any spectators."

*   *   *

"Captain," said a crew member of an intermediate orbiting station. "I've just picked up a tremendous power surge."

"Relay to the fleet," said the orbiter captain. "There should be no reactors of that magnitude there."

"Orbiter Five to Lucidulum. Reporting Sixth Magnitude surge."

*   *   *

"This is Fleet Commander Lucidulum. Ships Xrus-one and Chemeon-two, investigate power surge, Zone Twenty-Seven, over."

"On the way, sir, One and Two."

*   *   *

The robot turned to his glowing screen, on which two bright objects suddenly appeared. "Approaching starcraft, high velocity."

Micron popped up and down in his seat, straining against his safety belt. "Those are Lucidulum cruisers! They're after us!" He turned toward E.T.

E.T. lifted a finger. "We must—buzz off."

"We've got no food, no water!"

"We will find *junk food* along the way." E.T. hurried over to the radar screen, where the blips were getting bigger and louder.

"Now please—buzz off!"

Micron and the robot activated the command console, pressing many buttons, throwing all the levers. The door of the turnip slid closed.

"All secured."

"Main engines firing."

Outside the lizards watched, as the bottom half of the turnip lit up. The turnip seemed to hiccup off the ground; then suddenly it was lifted higher, camouflage blowing off it in a swirl of leaves.

Within the turnip, the robot continued to work his control board. "Second stage," he said, and his large round eyes began to fill with a grid of sparkling constellations, as his internal navigational mode came on.

E.T. went from place to place in the lattice work of Dagon Sabad, as the plant shot forth its power—streams of it flowing and feeding the rocketry of the Fusion Blooms. His turnip ship lifted rapidly now, into the night sky.

The robot switched on the outer viewing screens and the

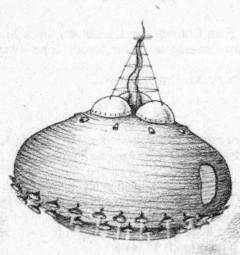

heavens appeared before them. Moving among the stars were two Lucidulum cruisers, rapidly approaching.

*   *   *

Botanicus and E.T.'s Parent sat together in the Parent's gourd. Upon the table before them was ambrosia Botanicus had brought, poured in crystalline cups whose pattern was a network of the distant stars in the constellation of Nahaz Erdu. They clicked their cups together, and the ten fingers of Botanicus glowed at the tips—his wisdom digits, one luminescence for each great deed he'd accomplished.

"Your child is unique, dear friend," he said. "He has always been my finest student."

The Parent sighed and sipped the ambrosia. "The Destiny Dreamers saw all this, of course, long ago. But it was thought better to keep it hidden."

The best decision," agreed Botanicus. "A great fate is hard enough, without being told of it in advance."

"And naturally," said the Parent, "one hopes that one's child will be spared, that he will remain ordinary, and consequently, happier."

Beside the beaker on the table was a transparent ball, showing the living night sky, stars twinkling. Botanicus leaned toward the ball, keenly interested, his ten fingertips radiant. "He found the power, he applied it correctly. And now—"

Streaking into view within the ball were the images of two Lucidulum starcruisers, and one flying turnip.

*   *   *

"Briiiiizz... starcraft closing fast." The robot's arms moved quickly, working his bank of controls. "I am setting course Six Seven Two, Near Moon Pass."

*   *   *

"Visual sighting, Captain, starboard."

"Aircraft specification, please," said the captain calmly, as he trimmed to starboard.

"It's—it's—"

"Yes? What did you say?"

"It appears to be a —I'm sorry, Captain, I—"

"Well, speak up, what is it?"

"A flying turnip, sir."

The starcruiser captain swallowed with some difficulty, and switched on his microphone, connecting him with the Commander of the Fleet.

"Starcruiser One reporting. In pursuit of Sixth Magnitude power emitter."

"Aircraft specification, please."

The starcruiser captain sighed, and made his report.

*   *   *

In the innermost chamber of Lucidulum, a startled voice rang out. "A flying *turnip?*"

"Yes, Your Lordship."

"The Commander of the Fleet is pursuing a vegetable?"

"Apparently so, Your Lordship. It appears to be some sort of hybrid."

A soft click on the central communication board sounded. "Commander, this is the Inner Chamber. You are pursuing a turnip?"

"Affirmative, Your Lordship."

"Do not fail to capture it, Commander. I'll not have our planet circumnavigated by members of the cabbage family."

"Circumnavigation is not its course, sir. It is already at the edge of our gravitational field and still accelerating."

"I don't care where it's going or how. You command the finest spacecraft in the galaxy. *Catch it.*"

A hatchway beneath each of the cruisers slid open, and as from the spinnerets of some great spider, lengths of super tensile line were spun out, and held by telescoping rods that joined the lines from cruiser to cruiser, in one great net, strong enough to hold a speeding comet.

Inside the turnip, Micron's fingers were flashing over his command console. The robot's metal fingers moved with equal precision at his navigation tasks. This was like the old days, when

he was a new machine, flying with the Fleet to the unknown—
when I was young, before they replaced me, before I became
outmoded.

He looked at the rear viewing screen, at the pursuing Fleet,
the Fleet that had scrapped him. "On course," he said, turning
to Micron. "We are headed into the Far Moon Pass."

E.T. looked into the view screen and saw the starcruisers
deploying their nets. They were trying to catch him, like a bug,
and pin his wings forever. He hurried over to the ring of Dagon
Sabad, and began to implore the plant to put forth more power.
"Please," begged E.T. "Show your stuff!"

To what end? asked the spirit of Dagon Sabad.

E.T. tried to answer, but no language from Earth or the stars
could describe what he felt. His heart alone glowed, and from it
came many vibrations—of a simple love he'd known, given by
a stranger in the universe, a boy, whose soul was somehow the
hope of the world. "His love is just a speck of dust in the ages,
Dagon Sabad, but I believe it is the only treasure."

Acceptable, said Dagon Sabad.

*   *   *

"Net formation stabilized."

The commander, leading the formation, gave the order. "Full
acceleration."

"Full power, Commander."

The net closed, encircling E.T.'s ship. But Dagon Sabad,
quickener of the Cosmic Egg, released a burst of Seventh Magnitude power, which it used for stirring sleeping nebulae.

At his viewing window, Micron saw the stars ahead cluster
and shift to the blue spectrum, as the turnip accelerated to light
speed and beyond.

"Briiiicck...we have escaped the net. Setting course, constellation Nahaz Erdu, Gate of Dimension."

I've just been outrun by a turnip, said the Commander of the
Star Fleet to himself.

"But I can't control it!" cried Micron, tilting off his seat and
dangling by his safety belt.

The turnip was wobbling, going into a spin, its walls beginning to shake. They had full power, of the Seventh Magnitude, but the untried ship, the experimental turnip, was unable to stand up to it.

E.T. fell down with the pitch and slid across the floor. His eyes rotated wildly, as the immensity of the power he'd tried to harness shook him from place to place. "El-li-ott!" he cried, knowing it was over, that his luck had failed, and that he'd dragged his innocent friends to their doom. The Flopglopple's face appeared next to his, as the creature joined him in sliding around.

"Forgive me," said E.T.

"...lovely time...sliding..." said the Flopglopple, for whom rolling over a waterfall in a broken barrel would be quite enjoyable, and pitching about in deep space in a rattling turnip was even better.

"We'll be killed!" cried E.T.

"Upside-down!" answered the Flopglopple, as the ship stood him on his head, where he balanced momentarily, toes in the air.

E.T. slid the other way across the floor, mind a net of anguish and regret. A telepathic surge went out from his brow, containing all that he knew from the collected centuries. It formed a telepathic replicant of tremendous vitality, his last gift to Elliott.

*   *   *

Elliott stood in the shadows of the dance floor. Julie was dancing with Snork Johnson.

"Guess he beat you out," said Tyler, standing next to Elliott.

"You think I care?" Elliott straightened the lapels of his jacket.

"Yeah," said Tyler, "I think you do."

"Well, you're wrong," said Elliott.

"Cut in on him," said Tyler. "Tell him to paddle off."

"I'm going downstairs," said Elliott, and went down the narrow staircase to the first floor of the rec hall, where the Ping-Pong tables were.

Lance was there, squinting across one of the tables. "Hey, Elliott, how's it going? Come on, I've got this table reserved."

Elliott sighed and picked up a paddle. This was his Friday night, playing Ping-Pong with the world's biggest nerd.

"Alright, Elliott, I've been perfecting my serve."

Elliott returned it lifelessly, not caring, the ball falling into the net.

"Brace yourself, Elliott, here comes a world class move."

E.T.'s replicant came through the ceiling, finally on target and streaking toward Elliott's head. It landed smoothly. Elliott felt a faint ripple pass through him and flicked his Ping-Pong paddle, sending the ball back at Lance with a table-edge hit that sent the ball over Lance's paddle and bounced it off Lance's forehead, between the eyes.

Elliott blinked, and tossed his paddle down. He walked across the rec hall to the steps and went up them. He walked onto the dance floor, and crossed over to Snork Johnson and Julie. Snork saw him and turned. "Get lost, shortstop," said Snork with a sneer, as he spun away.

Elliott stepped between him and Julie. "I'm cutting in," he said.

Snork curled his lip up, a superior remark beginning, dripping with sarcasm. And then his eyes met Elliott's, and what he saw there dissolved the words in his mouth. Because Elliott's eyes were filled with an uncanny presence, quite beyond anything Snork Johnson had ever seen. He turned and paddled away, wondering what had happened.

And Elliott turned to Julie.

"Hi," he said, as the next record came on over the speakers, a soft slow tune, which led them into each other's arms.

"Gee," she said, "you're a smooth dancer, Elliott."

*   *   *

"They're out of control, Commander," said the lead Lucidulum pilot. "We'll be able to overtake them again."

"Yes," said the Commander, "yes, I see. Deploy the nets once more." And to himself he thought, I will not be disgraced after all. I will not have to bear forever on my record that I was outrun by a flying turnip.

And he smiled to himself.

And then, inside the turnip, an odd thing happened:

At first E.T. thought it was a puncture in the shell of his ship. A curling wisp of fog floated in the air before him, resembling nothing so much as a large bulb of garlic. The bulb moved, semitransparent, ethereal, a walking cloud, toward the command console where Micron and the robot were struggling to maintain control of the turnip. The ghostly garlic bulb stood in beside Micron, and as it did so, it gained final shape, and its cloves unfolded with a metallic gleam, and long sinewy arms extended.

Don't get nervous, you sawed off transistor.

"Sinistro!" cried Micron.

The wraith smiled, and gestured, to a second wisp of ethereal substance forming in the room. *We've projected a bit of our mind power your way.*

The second wisp of mental stuff took shape on Micron's other side, and began hopping up and down like an excited toadstool.

"Electrum!"

At your service, said the old wraith, bending over the control board. Then beside him, a third wisp formed, like a mummy appearing from some buried chamber of the galactical tombs. It was Occulta's wraith, eyes burning with flames of yellow diamonds. *And now,* said his spectral voice, *let's trim this turnip.*

In the viewing screen, the Lucidulum Fleet appeared, drew closer, nets deployed. But Sinistro took over the controls, and Occulta and Electrum floated out onto the exterior surface of the turnip, where the Fusion rockets were blasting.

They separated, one to each side of the turnip, riding on its edge. Then they extended their arms, and a current leapt from their fingertips, sparkling and brilliant, and circled the turnip. Two of these magnetic rings they laid, like the frame of a gyroscope, the currents weaving, spinning, setting up a magnetic balance for the ship, and calming its fearful quaking.

From sun to sun, said Occulta, raising his arms to the stars, *let our rings be charged.*

Then he turned to the pursuing Fleet of Lucidulum and gave them a smiling wave, as their ships again fell behind in the chase, lost in the stabilized turnip's exhaust.

"On course," said the robot, inside. "Approaching constellation Nahaz Erdu, Gate of Dimension."

E.T. crawled to his feet, as the constellation appeared on the viewing screen, rushing toward them.

*   *   *

The soft song was slowly ending, as Elliott spun Julie to the center of the dance floor, beneath a big glass ball made of hundreds of tiny mirrors. The glass world turned slowly above them, reflecting the rainbow light of the hall, and Elliott drew Julie closer to him, and placed his lips on hers. The colors flashed, and in every facet of the turning world of glass Elliott and Julie were reflected in their first slow, perfect and unforgettable kiss.

*   *   *

And here we must leave you, said Sinistro, at the control board, and even as he spoke his ethereal substance began to fade, unable to enter the Gateway of Dimension. Sinistro became just a wisp of fog again, as did Occulta and Electrum.

"Mind projection fading," said the Flopglopple, as the wisps became no more than thin quivering plumes of disappearing crystals. But E.T. could hear, across the void, Electrum calling:

Don't forget my bicycle!

E.T.'s turnip ship entered the constellation of Nahaz Erdu, flying straight to the wormhole in its center, the Gateway of Dimension.

The turnip slipped from one time-space to another, and emerged at the second lap of its journey, in the Outer Sea of Light. Ahead were other wormholes, by which they would bridge the immensity of the universes, emerging ultimately in the Milky Way.

E.T. looked at his shipmates—Micron, the robot, and the Flopglopple—and held up two fingers, in the V-for-Victory sign he'd learned on Earth, his index finger glowing. And then, suddenly, the other finger lit up, signifying a great deed accomplished.

About the Author

William Kotzwinkle — novelist, poet, two-time recipient of the National Magazine Award for Fiction, and National Book Critics Circle Award nominee — is known for his broad range of style and subject. Among his noted works are *The Fan Man*, *Fata Morgana*, *Queen of Swords*, and *Doctor Rat*, winner of the World Fantasy Award. His stories have been included in *Great Esquire Fiction*, *Redbook's Famous Fiction*, and the *O. Henry Prize Stories*.